D0028974

Up a narrow flight I was suddenly in a space the size of the club below, illuminated only by a few security lights, but instead of a strip club, this was indeed a place where a magazine might be assembled. The sprawling office area had no cubicles and no sectioned-off smaller offices for managers. This was just a big, formerly empty area where a bunch of people who never put a magazine together before assembled to do so. Untidy desks with typewriters were at skewed angles everywhere, as were light tables and artist work stations. Brick walls wore bulletin boards thick with tacked-up photos and photo proof sheets, and book-filled board-and-block shelving straight out of a dorm room huddled under windows with blinds, not pink curtains—a sea of clutter that spoke of hard, energetic, even desperate work.

The hand on my shoulder made me jump.

I slipped my hand into my right windbreaker pocket, gripped the little gun and spun, ready to use it...

...and there stood Brandi Wyne in her curvy little blue-bikini glory, looking up at me with her big brown eyes and their big black pupils.

"I know what you're up to," she said...

QUARRY'S CLIMAX

by **Max Allan Collins**

A HARD CASE CRIME NOVEL

A HARD CASE CRIME BOOK
(HCC-130)
First Hard Case Crime edition: October 2017

Published by

Titan Books
A division of Titan Publishing Group Ltd
144 Southwark Street
London SE1 0UP

in collaboration with Winterfall LLC

Print edition ISBN 978-1-78565-180-9
E-book ISBN 978-1-78565-181-6

Design direction by Max Phillips
www.maxphillips.net

Typeset by Swordsmith Productions

The name "Hard Case Crime" and the Hard Case Crime logo
are trademarks of Winterfall LLC. Hard Case Crime books
are selected and edited by Charles Ardai.

Printed in the United States of America

Visit us on the web at www.HardCaseCrime.com

For Brian Van Winkle—
Quarry's brother-in-arms

*"There is nothing that will change
a person's moral outlook faster
than money in large amounts."*
LARRY FLYNT

*"I shall know the murderer
when I know the victim well."*
GEORGES SIMENON'S MAIGRET

OCTOBER 1975

ONE

I'd been doing murder for hire for five years now—well, seven and change, if you include the two tours in Vietnam. But in all that time, I'd never had a real, honest-to-God vacation. Unless you counted China Beach.

But this wasn't twenty miles of white sand in Da Nang perfect for sunning, surfing and suckee-fuckee. The war was over and this was Las Vegas, and you could get plenty of sun and suck-and-fuck here, but surfing in the Flamingo pool was probably not possible, even if you were a high roller who got comped.

Which I wasn't.

Not comped by the casino/hotel, that is. A pompous gent who called himself the Broker had paid for my room and anything I cared to charge to it, from meals to massage. So as vacations went, this was a winner. And it wasn't always easy to be a winner in Vegas.

But then this wasn't really a vacation, was it?

Next to the pool, on the sandstone apron, on a deck chair lapping up sun and letting his Ray-Ban-hidden eyes travel from one well-stuffed bikini to another was a slenderly muscular young man in his late twenties, nursing a tan with sunblock. He was good-looking in the kind of bland way that makes you forget his face almost immediately. His brown hair was short, but not military short; five ten, one-hundred-sixty pounds. He wore boxer trunks, dark blue, and he was me.

Oh, and in a nearby towel was wrapped a nine millimeter Browning. Just in case.

Someone settled into the deck chair to my left. Without looking, smelling the Brut aftershave, I knew who it was—my partner, and I don't mean romantically.

Boyd was small, no more than five six, but broad-shouldered enough to seem bigger—burly with a modest pot belly, curly brown hair infesting his head with the bushy eyebrows to go with it and an optional mustache and muttonchops. The rest of him was hairy, too, with only the black Speedo for relief. He also was wearing Ray-Bans.

"If they could only all be like this," he said.

He meant the job.

"Too many people," I said.

"You can get lost in a sea of people, Quarry."

"You can drown, too."

But at least he was in a good mood. The last job, Boyd had been glum as hell, after breaking up with his hairdresser boyfriend where he lived back east, though I didn't know exactly where that was. That was part of the Broker's arrangement—the two of us, teamed up for four years now, didn't even know each other's real names.

Like you're not going to know mine.

"My advice?" Boyd said, giving me a sideways glance, lifting and lowering the bushy brows like a bad Groucho imitation. "Let's milk it."

"You've already been here a week."

"This is your first day. Why not relax on the Broker's dime?"

Sun was lapping my face like a big friendly dog with a really warm tongue. "I don't relax on the job. That can get you killed."

"You're such a bummer sometimes."

That word, of course, was way out of date, and not used exactly right. But that was Boyd—a good half decade behind the curve. For a gay guy he could really be out of it sometimes.

"So, then…" He was looking at me with the bushy brows squinched together like fuzzy caterpillars mating. "…when do *you* want to go?"

The blonde I was looking at had lovely ass dimples rising above where her skimpy bikini cut across. She was almost plump, that wonderful way *Playboy* seemed to love.

"By 'go,' " I said, after taking a sip from the glass of Coke that was resting on a little marble-top table between us, "I assume you mean do the job. *After which* we will go. Promptly go."

The sigh came deep out of him, like a volcano letting out steam before erupting. "You are no fun, Quarry. No fucking fun *at* all."

"Never have been. Haven't you been paying attention?"

Instead of erupting, Boyd leaned toward me, his expression promising delight, like pudding bubbling on a stove.

"This is no ordinary job, my friend," he said. "We are in vacationland. Sin City. We are here under unusual circumstances, and should take advantage. How many times have we sat in rat-hole vacant apartments and lived like street bums?"

"If you're on the street, you're not in an apartment."

"You know what I mean! We're lucky when we wind up in a stakeout pad with Goodwill furniture, figure we're livin' like kings. This is the fucking Flamingo! Can't you just *enjoy* yourself for once?"

"It's work. It's a job. We're not supposed to enjoy it."

He patted the air, showing me palms that were among the few non-hairy areas of his flesh. Which put the lie to the old notion about what you got from jacking off.

"So, then, Quarry, what if we don't split right after the job? Why would we *have* to? In this case, who'd know the difference? It might even make a better cover for why we're here! Be less suspicious."

I just looked at him.

He made a sullen brat face and turned away and did some erupting inside himself.

The curvy brunette my eyes secretly followed seemed a party-pooper at first, because she was in a one-piece. But it clung to her so tight you could see every facet of her areolae and practically count the pubic hairs. The hair on her head was a gypsy tangle and the suit rode up over where her ass stopped being ass and became thighs. A few days in Vegas would be nice. Colorful beach umbrellas. Palm trees.

"I'll think about it," I said.

"Good! Great! Terrific! Why just *think*?"

"Well, thinking has worked out pretty well for me in the past."

"No, I mean, go with your *gut* for once!"

This was one of Boyd's problems, or anyway it was when he was between boyfriends, after a bad break-up. He thought with his gut, not his head. And of course his little head had its own ideas, which I really discouraged on the job. Pursuing his particular proclivities had risks. Of course, if he got himself killed off the job or something, that was up to him.

"We should clear it with the Broker," I said.

One beauty after another. You could spend all afternoon trying to spot cellulite and come up empty. And the sun! The damn sun. It *felt* yellow, turning your sweat to melted butter.

"Aw, Quarry—were you the kind of kid who asked Daddy's permission to take the car? Didn't you ever learn that it's less risky to apologize later than to ask up front?"

I didn't answer that one. He knew damn well I was a risk taker—granted, a calculated risk taker—but this conversation had gone on long enough.

Still, I understood his frustration. When he babbled on and

on about the shitholes that we sometimes got stuck with for surveillance, he had a right to bitch. He almost always worked the passive side of a job, going in ahead a week or two or more to establish the target's pattern of behavior, and to generally assess the lay of the land. Me, I was the active guy, who came in a day or two before the job, got filled in, did some minimal stakeout myself to get comfortable, then took out the target, quick and clean and painless as possible. I was not some sadistic schmuck.

We were both ex-military, former Vietnam, though Boyd had been there much earlier than me. That's who the Broker recruited for his network of professional killers…contract killers, if you insist, or—if you watch too much TV—hitmen.

I'd been a sniper and in that capacity took out thirty VC and at least that many more in firefights. I don't say "confirmed" kills because that's a bullshit term. Snipers filled out after-action reports that included kills "confirmed" by a second witness. But there's no official or unofficial "confirmed kill" record kept by the Marines, which was my branch.

Snipers worked with spotters (often the second witness mentioned above) and it was the same with the Broker's people. We worked in two-man teams, passive and active, and Boyd preferred the former and me the latter, which is why the stakeout conditions mattered to him.

And why Vegas was such a nice change of fucking pace.

I got that, but to me all these distractions were liable to, you know…distract.

I had moved in with Boyd in a two-bedroom suite that overlooked the pool and, beyond that, faced the rambling pastel-green building whose central section was four stories and whose wings were variously two- and three-stories—a mission-style castle built by that long-deposed king, Bugsy Siegel.

After flying from Mitchell airport in Milwaukee to McCarran here in Vegas, I took a cab to the nearest used-car lot to buy wheels for cash. Buying a piece of shit car to use on the job was my usual practice; I'd sell it back on the way out of town or dump it.

I'd had a busy enough day to crash for a few hours on a nice comfy double bed. The suite had light pink walls and darker pink everything else, and furnishings that were modern, if modern was twenty years ago.

I shat, showered and shaved, then joined Boyd in the living room. Sporting a salmon sports jacket, green turtleneck, green-and-black-and-white flared trousers and white loafers, my partner was seated on an Atom-age couch that looked a little less comfortable than the crate it was likely delivered in. *Happy Days* was on, having nothing to do with my youth. It was dark outside, a condition neon could only enhance, not defeat. I checked my watch—eight-fifteen. I'd slept a good long while.

Boyd filled me in on what he'd learned about our target. The timetable lacked the usual inconsistencies of behavior, because a schedule for our guy was built in. We were all set. Putting any more days between now and carrying out my end could not be justified, beyond the simple desire to live the good life in Vegas for a while.

And, like I said, this was not a vacation.

Of course, that didn't mean we had to live like monks. I got into the new shiny gray sharkskin suit, a black turtleneck and Italian loafers with no socks. We found our way to the Skyroom Restaurant with its westward view of the Caesars Palace fountains and various pulsing signage, the La Madre Mountains unable to compete without electricity. We took our time with a couple of filets, then let the casino have a shot at us, Boyd playing blackjack while I got to know one of these new video poker machines. I wound up five bucks ahead, playing quarters, while Boyd was down a couple hundred, at two bucks a pop. Finally we repaired to the Speakeasy Lounge.

The gangster-themed lounge boasted Joe-sent-me trappings, from flapper waitresses and bow-tie bartenders to fake brick walls with mounted machine guns and framed wanted posters. A friendly little place for fifty or sixty people to hang out—no cover and buck-twenty-five drinks, fifty-cent brews, free soda. We picked a table in back.

There were two acts. First was one of those bawdy busty broads who sang blue song parodies and told jokes that were shocking in 1955 ("Saturday night you girls sow wild oats, and Sunday morning you pray for a crop failure!"). She, the little card on the table said, went on at ten P.M., midnight and two A.M. She was just wrapping up her first show.

The audience was made up of more women than men, wives cooling their heels while their husbands gambled. The floating smoke was thicker and bluer than the raunchy gal's act, and the laughs from the well-oiled females were raspy in that aging Lucille Ball way.

Next up (eleven P.M., one A.M. and three A.M.) was Chicago boy Cliff Anthony, a road-company Sinatra who'd had one hit in the fifties ("Why Don't You Believe Me," a Joni James cover). He bounded out wearing a tux and confidence to the backing of a five-piece combo and didn't loosen his tie till halfway through the second song. He was handsome in a puffy kind of way with hair as black as India ink; a typically small Italian crooner, he was nonetheless sturdy-looking, though his moves were like a compact car trying to get around a truck.

I guess he wasn't bad, but it annoyed me that every time he sang somebody else's song ("The Lady Is a Tramp," "Beyond the

Sea," "Volare") he would pause to get the audience to applaud, like it was his goddamn hit. I don't know which irritated me more, the way he was milking a cow that didn't belong to him or how the dumb-ass crowd applauded on cue.

"I got a couple of his albums at home," Boyd whispered during an instrumental break in "The Candy Man."

"That right."

He gave me a squinty-eyed look. "Don't you like this kind of stuff? Or are you strictly into that Beatles shit?"

Boyd thought the Beatles were the latest thing. If I'd said I liked Blondie, he'd have thought I was talking about the funny papers.

"Well," I said magnanimously, "at least it's not disco."

"What's wrong with disco?"

That trend he was up on!

A woman wearing half a tube of lipstick and with more wrinkles than a shar pei shushed us. Boyd made a face and sipped his ginger ale. I sipped my Coke. Anthony was getting credit for "Danke Schoen" now.

During "Tie a Yellow Ribbon," Boyd said, "You know, they love him in Chicago."

"He's flat everywhere. Riding the cracks in the piano."

"Maybe so, but he works one week a month here, and the rest of the time in little clubs all over the Windy City."

"Don't call it that."

"What?"

"Nobody from Chicago calls it the Windy City."

He shrugged. "Yeah, well, I'm not *from* Chicago. Anyway, he does a ton of weddings and bar mitzvahs there, too."

The shar pei with lipstick was giving us a dirty look.

Boyd nodded toward the stage. "See that cauliflower-ear character down front? Table for one?"

"Yeah. That's the evening-shift guy?"

"That's him. None of them are Outfit. Just guys our boy plucked out of this bar or that one. Bouncers. Think at least one goes back to high school days. Football buddies."

"Rah yay team."

As if we'd requested it, the lounge lizard started in on "My Kind of Town." That was enough for me. Had to get out of there before "New York, New York." I rose, curled my finger at Boyd, who pouted but followed me reluctantly out.

"What now?"

I checked my watch. "You need a nap or anything?"

"What am I, six?"

"Lose some more money, if you want. I'm gonna go back to the room and relax. Watch some TV."

He gave me a silly grin. "They got porn."

"What am I, sixteen?"

Shrug. "I'll play a while. When you want me back?"

"Five. It'll still be dark."

He nodded, then strolled off into the midnight sun of a dinging and clanging world that waited to take more of his money. I had a little work to do, spending half an hour checking out the underground parking garage, where I found what I was looking for, right where it was supposed to be.

In our suite, I put *Chinatown* on our room tab, and then *Young Frankenstein*. I'd seen them both before, but they were good. During "Puttin' on the Ritz," I fell asleep on the sofa, even though I'd had enough Coca-Cola caffeine to fly back to McCarran.

What woke me was Boyd coming back in. The night latch was on, so I got up and let him in. I stopped off at the john to get rid of some of that Coke, the pause that really refreshes, and joined him in the living room.

"Pack your shit," I told him, "and take mine, too." My travel bag was ready to go. "Be in your car with the motor running at six-fifteen. I parked up top. It's a beater, so if we have to haul ass, we can leave it behind."

"You wipe the car down for prints?"

"No, I made sure to leave every clue I could. Your picture's in the glove compartment with the bill of sale for my nine mil."

He laughed at that, said, "Sorry."

I took off my suitcoat and got into the shoulder holster with the silenced nine millimeter Browning in it. Rarely did I wear a rig like that, but sticking the bulky gun in my waistband just wouldn't cut it. Even at this time of night, or morning or whatever, too many people would be around.

"Gun doesn't show at all," Boyd said admiringly, eyes on my right shoulder.

"The Broker recommended a tailor," I said. "Paid for it himself."

Boyd smirked. "Isn't this the goddamnedest job?"

"It is. And I wish it were over."

"Will be, soon enough."

"Guy ever had a girl in there, this time of day?"

"No."

"Sure about that?"

"Now who's asking stupid questions, Quarry? Strictly an afternoon delight type. Too wiped after work for funtime. Quick bite of breakfast at the in-house café, and off to beddy-bye."

"And only the one bodyguard?"

"Well, like I said earlier, there's three…but they work one at a time. Guy there now does the five A.M. to one P.M. shift. So he just went on—he'll be alert."

"Not for long."

I went to the window for a look. Despite the hour, the pool

was still doing a good business, more bikini girls parading in the reflective glow. The round umbrellas were like big colorful poker chips and the squat palms lent an exotic vibe.

In the sprawling Mission-style building on the other side of the pool, mobster Bugsy Siegel and his moll, Virginia Hill, had lived and fought and fucked in the penthouse suite on the top floor of the central four stories. According to Boyd, Siegel haunted the penthouse, now known as the Presidential Suite, where the man who "invented" Las Vegas dwelt while he built the Flamingo.

"Guests stayin' in that suite," Boyd had reported to me over dinner, between bites of rare filet mignon, "tell of strange run-ins with Bugsy's ghost—and *cold* spots that give you the *shivers*... plus, things that were left *here* and wind up *there*."

"Yeah," I'd said. "There's a name for poltergeists like that— housekeeping."

He ignored that, caught up in the around-the-campfire moment. "They've seen his ghost all around the place—in a bedroom, and in the living room, standing by the pool table."

"So how *is* ol' Bugsy these days?"

"Except for being dead, Quarry, apparently not bad! Doesn't seem unhappy or out of sorts. Must be pleased to still be around the place."

"Maybe he's getting a charge out of seeing how his dream played out."

"Maybe! Kinda all came true, didn't it?"

"Yeah. Course, he probably didn't dream of getting shot full of holes in his girlfriend's living room."

In a corner of the underground parking garage, itself a relic of the early days of the casino/hotel, a door waited that wore its age without dignity, a somewhat warped affair, its face a paint-peeling mess worthy of Dorian Gray. The Flamingo, despite occasional signs of its long run here on the Strip, was relatively spiffed up. This was like a big rectangular scab in the corner.

But the key the Broker provided worked fine. I did not lock the door behind me, since the need for a quick Bugsy-style getaway remained a possibility—like if one bodyguard turned into three. The promised light switch inside the door at right clicked the long cement corridor into a weak state of jaundice, thanks to bare yellow bulbs in the ceiling spotted along every ten feet or so. This was the kind of passageway that led to an electric chair back in the old days. And in some states still did.

About eight light bulbs down I came to another door, the slightly better-preserved twin of the previous one, and no key was required. Steep stairs awaited, cement again—no creaking to announce me. They led to three landings, the third of which had a ladder—bare wood but of a vintage going back decades—leaned against the wall opposite.

I was still in the gray suit with the black turtleneck. But the silenced Browning was in my surgical-gloved right hand now, as I scaled the ladder to a panel in the ceiling.

Well, sort of in the ceiling. Actually in the floor of the room above. And that room was the penthouse, the front closet of which I pulled myself up and into. Only a few coats hung—the climate required a raincoat or two, one topcoat reserved for weird weather, but mostly just empty hangers for me not to bump into.

With the lid leaned against a side wall, I sat there in the opening, legs dangling like a kid in a high chair, and braced myself in case my minimal noise had roused anybody.

Apparently it hadn't.

Straddling the square hole in the floor, I used my left hand to work the doohickey on this side of the closet-opening knob. Turning that worked just fine, and I got the door open quickly, ready to deal with the bodyguard in the front room.

The fairly narrow but very long living room had, as promised, a pool table taking up a good third of it. I was facing the table now. At my left, at the far end, was a wet bar. A wall of windows, straight ahead, looked out onto the pool, curtains back, night not having given in to morning yet, dawn not even a threat.

But the expected bodyguard was nowhere to be seen in this considerable space.

Then, from behind a door next to me, came a flush. I positioned myself with my back to the wall next to that door. Next came the sound of running water. He was a good employee, washing his hands like that. Probably made drinks and handled food for his boss. He deserved a gold star.

He got it. When he came lumbering out—another cauliflower-eared ex-bouncer with eyes peering out of slits and an open mouth waiting for a thought to form—I clubbed him along the right side of his head with the noise-suppressed nine mil. He immediately transformed into a useless pile of protoplasm, and I caught him with my free arm, to lower him gently to the pink pile carpet.

His heavy breathing meant the blow hadn't killed him, at least not just yet, and I used the duct tape in my suitcoat pocket to secure his wrists behind him and his ankles together, and just for good measure slapped some across his mouth, getting a little drool on my hand that I wiped off on his leisure suit jacket—a plaid number from the Who Shot the Couch collection. No gun. Some bodyguard.

I checked the place, knowing the layout well from the provided materials. The two bathrooms off the living room were unpopulated. The guest bedroom, too. The living room had painted plaster walls, but the first bedroom I checked sported pink-and-black vertical-striped wallpaper, the pink parts shiny, the stripes wide. The bed was a king with a pink spread and matching fluffy pillows.

The master bedroom was larger but similar, the main differences being black-and-shiny-gold-striped wallpaper and a big round bed.

Cliff Anthony, in black silk pajamas, the top unbuttoned onto a hairless, pudgy chest, was on his back on top of the black-and-gold spread, snoring, dead to the world.

I sat on the bed and bumped up and down a little, till it woke him up.

Feminine eyelashes in the masculine face fluttered like spooked butterflies. "*Huh!* Huh?"

"Good morning, Starshine. That's from *Hair*—the hit's by a guy named Oliver, not that you'd ever mention that."

He propped himself on his elbows. "Who the fuck…?"

"Think of me as Jiminy Cricket with a gun." I pressed the nose of the silenced automatic against his forehead, some greasy black locks fringing down. I gave it some muscle, dimpling his deeply tanned flesh.

"What the fuck…?"

"Sam is unhappy."

"Oh, fuck…"

"Been banging his teenage daughter, haven't you, Cliff? Oh, she's of age, but he's still not pleased."

"Oh Jesus…"

"You have friends in Chicago who asked Sam if he might reconsider sending someone like me."

Shaking his head, as if trying to clear it, he said, "I'll never touch her again! I swear on my Mama's grave. Never, *never* touch her again!"

I shot the pillow next to him, which even noise-suppressed made it plump up some and spit feathers, the sound a substantial pop/click.

Anthony's eyes were wide, his hands up, palms out. The front of his pajama bottoms was damp.

"If I come back here," I said, and pushed the nose of the weapon under his chin for a little emphasis, "my aim will improve."

He was shivering and crying as I left him.

I thought about going out the front way but, just in case I did have to come back here one of these days, I took the closet route, using the ladder and replacing the panel.

When I emerged from the corner doorway in the underground garage, Boyd was behind the wheel of his car, a Chevy Caprice convertible; he almost always rented, a risk I never took.

"Well?" he asked, bright-eyed as a deer about to get run down.

Getting in on the rider's side, I said, "No rush. We're fine. But I almost killed the motherfucker, despite Broker's orders."

"What? Why?"

"Prick wouldn't sign an album to you!"

Boyd laughed out loud at that. "Quarry, you're a card. A regular joker."

"This is the town for it," I said. "Drive."

TWO

Paradise Lake in October really lives up to its name.

First, God or Mother Nature or whoever-the-fuck-is-in-charge does a bang-up job on the fall colors—red, gold, yellow, amber, a forest fire that never gets out of hand. The trees, fat with leaves in their colorful death throes, crowd the placid blue of the lake to reflect back at themselves in strange but lovely abstract shapes, the sky adding streaks of white to its own blue reflection.

Second, there are no tourists. For me having a minimum number of people around is about as close to heaven as Wisconsin gets. I don't mind the spring and summer, when the hordes invade, because a good number of those are female and young and looking for fun and no commitment. And have they found the right guy.

But mindless sex gets old after four or five months, and when the outsiders give way and I'm only dealing with the handful of locals who tolerate me much as I tolerate them, lack of pussy becomes almost a relief. I have some pretty good friends in nearby Lake Geneva who, like me, are professionals, though their professions are rather more dull, like being a lawyer or a doctor or a successful merchant. We play poker for low stakes—quarter, fifty-cents, a buck—and give each other a good-natured hard time. They envy me because I am a little younger and they're aware of that young pussy I mentioned.

Still, every one of them has a loving wife, each quite attractive, and kids who don't hate them, which is novel. There's much to be envied about their boring lives. And anyway who am I to talk? Much of my life is more boring than theirs. I only do half a dozen jobs a year, tops, and the rest of the time I just loaf around my lakeside A-frame watching television and reading paperback westerns and spy novels. When the weather isn't right for swimming in the lake, I go to a health club in Lake Geneva and swim there. And in college-girl off-season, I hang out at the Playboy Club in Geneva, where I've gotten to know a number of waitresses very well. That's Bunnies to you. In case you were wondering what kind of man reads *Playboy*.

My poker buddies think I'm a lingerie salesman (which leads to considerable joshing) alternating travel with supervising other salesmen from home.

So it's a quiet life, dull and out of the way, but on the rare instances where the Broker drops by, life seems suddenly lively.

Not that the Broker is a terribly lively individual. Nor does he actually "drop by"—on my weekly touch-base calls, from a pay phone, he very occasionally announces that he would "like to arrange a visit on your premises." Yes, he really does talk that way. And by "occasionally," I would say his visits to my "premises" numbered maybe five times in as many years. Usually we met at restaurants, often truck stops, and sometimes at the hotel he owned in Davenport, Iowa.

I first met him a few months after I came home from the Nam, as we called that hellhole. Despite all the carnage I'd endured and delivered, I had returned to the Good Ol' U.S. of A. with a streak of naivete still in my genes, and for that matter my jeans. I had married a lovely little California type who an Ohio kid like me had thought existed only in my own mind when I listened to the Beach Boys crooning "Surfer Girl." A quick courtship before I went overseas, and an exchange of many tender letters between us, did not prepare me for (yeah, I know, you're way ahead of me) finding Joni in bed with some other guy.

A quick tip to returning-home military men: never show up a day early.

Maybe you've also guessed I didn't take it well, but you might be surprised to learn that I restrained myself. I didn't kill either one of them, right then. But after a long soul-searching night, I went over to the guy's house in La Mirada to talk it out. But right off the bat, he called me a bunghole and—he was working under his little sports car at the time—I kicked out the fucking jack.

Ultimately the death was declared accidental, though they almost tried me and the papers got some real play out of it. Maybe it got some national coverage too, because I figure that's how the Broker tracked me down. He found me in a nasty part of L.A., feeling sorry for myself, the only time in my relatively young life that I was ever on a bender. I normally drink in moderation. That's not sarcasm. Coca-Cola's my chief vice.

The Broker, for all his pomp, knew how to take advantage of my circumstance. He understood that I resented having been paid and even honored by my country for killing a bunch of yellow people for no fucking reason in particular and then getting vili-fucking-fied for murdering a single goddamn white son of a bitch who had it coming. I guess I hadn't figured out the life-isn't-fair part.

This was my home turf—my premises, right?—so I did not make any effort to make myself presentable to the Broker. He was due to arrive late afternoon and he would have to accept me in the Wisconsin sweatshirt, jeans, and sneakers I'd been wearing all day. I lived alone—my little blue heeler, Pooch, had died last year, something I'm not really over to this day—and I was not about to suck up to the guy. Not that I ever had.

On the other hand, the A-frame was as neat as a Marine's

footlocker. I don't like to live in a mess. There's a big central room with a fireplace and some sectional couches, a loft overlooking it where the 25" TV and a Barcalounger live, and a kitchenette with a long counter and new appliances. Several bedrooms are down the hall and there's one bathroom.

The knock at the front door came at four P.M. He was on my doorstep looking like a bank president who had lost his way to his country club's golf course. He was tall, six-two, with broad shoulders on a trim frame, his tan making the icy blue eyes stand out, as did the white eyebrows and mustache that went with his prematurely white hair, worn longish like all the old farts were doing.

But *was* he an old fart? I never could get a fix on his age. He might be forty and he might be sixty. His long, narrow face had few wrinkles, as if he hadn't used it much for anything but eating and maybe breathing. As for why he might have been on his way to the links, he was wearing a dark brown suede sport coat, bronze turtleneck, gray-and-black-and-brown plaid flares, and brown hush puppies, a matching bronze handkerchief in his breast pocket.

All he lacked was a five-iron to lean on.

"Quarry," he said, voice radio-announcer resonant, and held his hand out for me to shake.

I did. It was a firm clasp, no moisture, a little cool, like greeting a statue.

Looking past him at my little blacktop driveway, I noted that his latest Cadillac—the same arctic blue as his eyes, a custom color I'd wager—did not have a driver.

"You're alone?" I asked.

"Yes. Quite alone."

Is there a difference between "alone" and "quite alone"? You tell me.

I ushered him in.

"Lovely drive up here." He'd come from the Iowa/Illinois Quad Cities most likely, since his home base was his hotel. "Simply alive with color."

Well, all those leaves were dying, but I understood what he meant.

He was taking the lead down the short hall and I was following, frowning at his back. He almost never went anywhere without one of his...one of his what? Bodyguards? Protégés? These were young men, Vietnam vets like me mostly, who seemed to be in training for something—possibly the kind of work I did.

Sometimes I suspected a sexual aspect, but I had heard from Boyd that the Broker had a beautiful young wife and also that he was known to fool around with other (to use a Broker-ish phrase) "willing wenches."

"We could sit on the deck," I said, gesturing to the sliding glass doors. "But it'll start getting cold any time now."

"We'll stay inside," he said. He settled onto the sectional couch, facing the black metal fireplace.

"Coors all right?"

"Please."

I got myself one too and delivered his, and sat on the couch section angled to his left. I sipped the beer, then set it on a coaster on the low-slung glass-topped coffee table.

I asked, "Problem with the job?"

Vegas had been last week.

He raised a hand like a kid in class. "No, no! All the feedback has been positive."

"A little soon for another contract, isn't it?"

He seemed distracted. He was staring at the fireplace as if the flames were making particularly interesting patterns and shapes. Only there wasn't a fire going in it.

"It's…" Tiny sigh. "…I find myself facing a particularly unusual situation, Quarry."

He gave me the name "Quarry," by the way. He said I reminded him of something carved out of rock. It was a kind of code name, but I also sometimes used it as an alias on the job. I had several driver's licenses with Quarry as a last name. Anyway.…

"The last job," I said, "was unusual enough. You don't usually pay me *not* to kill somebody."

He smiled a little, still distant, not looking at me. Staring at the nonexistent fire.

"Quarry, perhaps you've noticed that I've come to lean on you when the circumstances are…unusual…unique. When someone with the ability to do more than just bring violence to bear is called for."

"Yeah," I said.

And I *had* noticed that. More than a few times, he'd sent me in undercover, having me gather up-close-and-personal intel, among other (as he said) unusual or unique assignments that went beyond simply hitting some fucker. Like the Vegas gig, for example.

Now he looked at me, head swiveling on his neck but the rest of him still facing forward. His gaze was hard and unblinking, yet somehow it revealed a human being back behind there. Not an exemplary human being perhaps, possibly a sociopath and certainly a twisted and self-interested one. But human.

"You have exceptional instincts, Quarry. You knew at once that my coming unaccompanied bore significance."

Now he was just blowing smoke up my skirt. Anybody with half a brain—Boyd, say—would have read the Broker's solo appearance as a red flag.

"Fuckin' A," I said. "I'm special. Like the kids on the short bus. What's this about, anyway?"

He sipped beer. Placed the can on a coaster. Studied the non-fire. Swung the ice blues my way; they tightened, like screws turning.

"I recently declined a contract," he said.

I thought about that for a second or two, then shrugged. "I'd imagine you do that fairly often."

"Yes, but this time the reason *why* I declined the job required obfuscation on my part."

Every time I talked to this pompous motherfucker, he laid a word on me I'd never heard in conversation before.

"Okay," I said. "I think that means you lied to whoever offered the job about why you took a pass."

He nodded. "Precisely. Because the real reason would not have gone over well."

Jesus! Did I have to drag each thought out of him?

"Why was that, Broker?"

He swallowed. The eyes relaxed, or maybe surrendered. "Because this was a contract on someone I do *not* wish to see killed."

Again, I thought for a few moments—maybe more than a few—then said, "I might know where this is going…"

He raised a hand. Collected his thoughts. I'd never seen him like this.

"Quarry, as you might well imagine, I have many dealings and investments that are, let us say, outside the realm of the business in which you and I are engaged. Some are what are colloquially termed 'money laundries,' while others are simply profitable concerns. Money-makers."

"Okay."

He sighed. "Before I continue with this line of talk, I must ask you to take a deep breath and contemplate. You see, this is outside the agreement we made some years ago in a sleazy apartment in the Skid Row of Los Angeles. This requires you to enter with me into a dangerous domain that carries with it potentially dire consequences."

"How does it pay?"

That made him smile, just a little, the mustache going along for the ride. "It will pay exceptionally well. Twenty-five thousand now, twenty-five after, and all expenses are mine. I will be able to pave your way along the path…a treacherous path, but one I have confidence that you can navigate."

I squinted at him, as if seeing him better would bring him into focus. "But if you tell me what this is, I can't turn it down, right? I *have* to sign on."

"Yes. Eyes wide open…but blind, so to speak."

I thought a while. Shrugged. "It's good money. Risks don't bother me, unless they're stupid. Shoot. So to speak."

He took in a deep breath and let it out. Now his torso swiveled to me and his expression was faintly, very faintly, smiling. "Are you familiar with a particularly tasteless publication called *Climax*?"

Of course I was. I read every monthly issue. It had very funny vulgar cartoons, an acid pox-on-all-your-houses political slant, and had broken barriers and taboos by publishing naked beauties with their legs spread and sharing a view of what had heretofore only been available to their gynecologists and maybe their lovers. Lately a bunch of court cases had put *Climax* in the headlines, the editor/publisher facing obscenity charges.

"Vaguely," I said with a shrug. "Raunchy skin mag, isn't it?"

The white eyebrows raised and lowered in the tan face. "To say the least! I certainly had no idea it would become a success in its field, let alone a *cause célèbre*."

I sat forward. "You say that like you had something to do with it."

He sighed. His expression was one I'd never seen from him before. What was it? Shit! *Embarrassment!* The Broker was embarrassed!

"Just because I might invest in a hamburger chain," he said somewhat stiffly, "does not necessarily mean such cuisine is to my taste."

"You're an investor. You backed *Climax*."

One-shoulder shrug. "Several of us did. It began as a money laundry but turned unexpectedly profitable. This man in Memphis was poor white trash, as they say, but he displayed a genius for making bars and strip clubs pay. He became so successful at it that he began talking about expanding into the magazine field. The conditions were ideal for passing money through, as all of us felt the chances of his success in an already crowded arena were minimal." The Broker rolled his eyes. "Then he came up with his grand idea of depicting women in all their hirsute glory, and the money began to *stream* in!"

"Max Climer," I said. "That's his name, right?"

I knew damn well it was his name. In just a year or so, he had become as famous as *Playboy*'s Hugh Hefner and *Penthouse*'s Bob Guccione.

"That's indeed his name."

I was frowning again. "You said you turned down a contract. So who did Climer want killed?"

The Broker's hands flew up like Butterfly McQueen in *Gone With the Wind* crying Lawsy-mercy. "No one! There are those who want *him* killed."

I gaped at him. "*Climer's* the contract you turned down?"

"Yes. Yes."

I sat back. "Who wants him dead?"

"I have no idea."

I dealt him half a smirk. "Broker. Remember who you're talking to."

"I have no idea, Quarry!" He heaved a weight-of-the-world sigh worthy of Atlas himself. "You must understand, son. The business I'm in…the business *we're* in…is multi-layered, designed to protect all concerned. Including ourselves. Insulation every step of the way. You never know who hired you. Neither, in most cases, do I."

I was shaking my head. "Hard to buy, Broker."

"Perhaps." The eyebrows flicked up and down. "And I… *generally* know the, shall we say, direction from which a contract is coming. Most often it's from the nationwide crime syndicate—various factions thereof, that is. And remember that the straight citizens who seek our help most often do so through someone they've encountered along their mostly lawful way who operate in the left-handed endeavor of organized crime. Many respectable businessman—captains of industry included—have turned to such sources for financing at times. And, networking through those sources, they turn to us for the removal of inconvenient associates, or troublesome personal ties."

What he meant was business partners or rivals, and wives or mistresses or the lovers thereof. Thereof! Now he had me doing it.

The Broker flipped a hand. "Those who might like to see Max Climer depart from the ranks of the living are numerous and varied. A veritable legion."

That seemed a silly exaggeration, even for this pretentious prick.

I said, "Come on, Broker—surely you can work backward through your contacts, discreetly, and come up with the client you rejected."

"Possibly," he admitted. "But I must not do anything that

might lead back to me. The ramifications would be unfortunate and severe. The entire network of professionals like yourself and Boyd would be endangered. No, I can't go through the back door—*you* must find a window."

I sipped Coors. "Well, if you're looking for ideas...Boyd and I could go to Memphis...Climer still operates out of there, right, his clubs and his magazine?"

The Broker nodded.

I went on: "Boyd and I could stake out this Climer joker and see if somebody else is doing the same. We might be able to take out the hitters. Should be able to. But that doesn't take care of the *bigger* problem—whoever wants Climer dead will just try again. Hire someone else."

His lips twitched and his mustache bristled. "Your analysis is inarguable."

That meant he agreed, I guessed.

The arctic eyes froze mine. "Your job will be to stop the impending assassination of this pornographer and to determine who put it in motion."

"By stop it, you mean kill the team sent to do the job?"

He gave one small nod.

"And," I said, "by determining who put it in motion, you mean kill the son of a bitch who hired it?"

Another small nod.

"I'm not sure I know how to do that," I said. "Boyd and I can track another team—that's tricky but doable. But how can I be expected to find out who hired it when somebody as connected as you can't?"

"*Won't*," he corrected me. "As I explained, I don't dare. It would risk—"

"Yeah, I got that. But it gets back to the insulation concept. Assuming the hitters are pros, they probably work like Boyd and me, like *all* your guys—meaning they have no contact with whoever hired them."

He was nodding, slowly. "I believe—call it an educated guess—that someone close to the pornographer will be the client. I have already provided Boyd with a list of names with photos and rundowns of those I suspect. He'll obviously share that intelligence with you."

I frowned. "Wait, you've already talked to Boyd? You went to him first?" Somehow that seemed insulting. My feelings were a little hurt. I was the number one guy on the two-man team—right? Right?

He sensed my reaction. "Quarry, Boyd is considerably more malleable than you. I knew you would be sharper, shrewder, and would require a more detailed, sophisticated sell."

More smoke up my skirt. But it felt kind of good.

"I also knew," he went on, "that if Boyd was on board, your loyalty to your partner would be a factor in my favor. You would not want to subject him to some stranger as a partner—not in facing so delicate and dangerous a task. Nor would you want to deny your associate the chance for so handsome a payday. You have too great a sense of honor."

Okay, now that was a little too much smoke.

"How is having rundowns on the suspects helpful," I said, "when Boyd and I are sitting stakeout?"

"No need for both of you to take the passive end, not at all times. You'll take active, as usual. But I've arranged to get you inside the *Climax* organization. You see, I've been able to suggest to Mr. Climer that he may have a quisling in his wood-pile."

"I know what's usually in a Southern white guy's woodpile, but what the fuck is a quisling?"

His eyes narrowed. "A betrayer. A traitor. I've seen to it that you have been recommended by an associate of mine to Mr. Climer as a minder."

"A what?"

"A guardian. A defender. A bodyguard, if you will."

Like the guy in Vegas who I duct-taped into submission. Only with a gun.

"So I work from the inside again," I said.

"You are the only one of my boys I would trust with such an assignment. Such a responsibility."

"Right, 'cause I'm unique and shit."

He smiled small and shrugged big.

I sighed. Narrowed my eyes at him. "Fifty for stopping the hit from going down," I said, "and another fifty for the guy behind it."

He took a moment to consider that, and another nod, more definite, followed.

"You can tell Boyd it's a go," I said.

The Broker stood, smoothed his suede jacket. "You can tell him yourself, Quarry. He's already in Memphis...would you like to join me at the Lake Geneva Playboy Club for supper? I'm a key holder."

So was I, but he didn't need to know how sophisticated I really was. I got into more respectable attire and let him buy me a meal. When we were served by a Bunny who I'd dated and banged, I kept it to myself.

He didn't have a corner on all the secrets.

THREE

I flew out of Mitchell in Milwaukee again, a ninety-minute flight to Memphis International. As was my habit, I took a cab to the nearest sketchy-looking used car dealership, where I could pay cash and get title to match my phony ID (John R. Quarry) no questions asked. The sunny if humid weather encouraged me to go a little flashy, so I paid two grand of the Broker's money for a pale green '69 Mustang convertible.

The ride to downtown Memphis, mid-afternoon, took only twenty minutes. I'd been here before, on one of my first jobs for the Broker, but that was almost five years ago. The area was still mostly a desolate, boarded-up place whose hard times had gotten harder after the murder of Martin Luther King; but it was starting to work its way back. I parked on South 2nd and, in my gray t-shirt, jeans and tennies, strolled to the Rendezvous and the best ribs in town, after which I walked it off on the riverfront.

That took me through Tom Lee Park, where a massive new bridge with M-shaped arches loomed. The gray shimmer of the Mississippi was undisturbed but for a paddlewheeler brimming with tourists. Tom Lee, by the way, was an African-American dock worker who saved the lives of thirty-two passengers when a steamboat sank in 1925. If that paddlewheeler started to go down, the odds of me diving in to start saving people weren't so good. I mean, I'm a hell of a swimmer, but I would never dream of stealing Tom Lee's thunder.

I retrieved my Mustang and headed for the address the Broker had provided, which was a bit of a head-scratcher. That years-ago Memphis job had taken me to the Highland Strip before, to remove a drug dealer (presumably for one of his competitors), and that the area might include a budding publishing empire seemed hard to fathom.

The Highland Strip had been a virtual extension of the University of Memphis campus for a very long time. Last trip I'd been told that before the late sixties, Highland Street near Southern Avenue had been a typical shopping district—grocery, hardware, jewelry store, barber shop and so on. What pulled the students in was a record store called Pop-I's, where campus hippies began to gather. Soon funky restaurants, head shops and clothing stores began popping up, boutiques like Sexy Sadie and the Jeanery, restaurants like the Taj Mahal and The Café, plus The Cue Ball, a pool hall with an opium-den vibe. By the time of my visit here five years ago or so, the Highland Strip was strictly a hangout for freaks, longhairs, tie-dye tees, bell bottoms, and bare feet.

But as my Mustang prowled the Strip of today, with afternoon trailing into dusk, I saw a mix of empty boarded-up storefronts and new businesses, conventional ones not unlike the ones the hippies had driven out. College kids still walked the streets, but they just looked like students, not users looking to make a connection.

My destination turned out to be another defunct store in this neighborhood trying to work its way back to normalcy. The faded red-brick building was two stories, the white-paint-lettered ghost of CAFÉ floating above boarded-up double doors between plywood-covered storefront windows.

On the corner directly opposite was a three-story tan-brick building whose bottom floor, under a dark brown overhang, bore a fieldstone facade with beer neons glowing in its windows. Above the overhang, a sign extended from the side of the building like an arm signaling a turn, with red neon pulsing

CLIMAX CLUB, smaller letters saying COCKTAILS. This substantial but hardly ostentatious structure did not look like the home of either a publishing empire or a nightclub that might have inspired one. But that's exactly what it was.

I parked the Mustang, putting up its top, on the street around the corner from the stakeout. The apartment over the dead café was accessed on the cross-street side of the building. The door was locked, but I had a key courtesy of the Broker. Travel bag in hand, I went up unlit, creaky, musty stairs to a claustrophobic, equally creaky landing, and knocked three times, like Tony Orlando but louder.

Footsteps behind the old paint-peeling door came my way and stopped.

"Me," I said to the paint-peeling wood.

Boyd peeked out, confirmed my claim, and let me in.

"Welcome to my world," he said with a sour smirk, scratching his head of curly brown hair.

This wasn't a room at the Flamingo.

We stood in something that had been a kitchen, and, as if to prove it, an old refrigerator hummed in wheezy indignation about having to stay at it after so many loyal years of service, while blistered white cabinets hovered over a once-white counter like suspects in a lineup. A gray Formica table with paint stains and a couple of gold-and-gray chairs, their vinyl upholstery splitting, completed the less-than-inviting display; all the other appliances were missing in action, their shadows on the wall as if in the aftermath of an A-bomb.

Boyd was in a ribbed red long-sleeve shirt and black-and-red plaid pants. He surveyed the scene like an alien who had landed in the midst of ancient ruins.

His mouth pursed beneath his mustache. "Why do we put up with this shit?"

I shrugged. "The money? Rest of the joint this inviting?"

"Take the tour and see."

The place was, or had been, a furnished apartment. A hallway off the kitchen fed two bedrooms to the left, each with a double bed and an excuse for a nightstand. With a shiver, Boyd said that the mattresses had been bare and he'd gone to J.C. Penney and got us sheets and blankets and pillows. Sometimes having a gay partner comes in handy.

I stowed my travel bag in the unclaimed bedroom; between it and Boyd's quarters was a working john with a shower stall, which was the pad's only redeeming feature. Someone had cleaned it, almost certainly Boyd.

The living room seemed spacious, or maybe that was just because it had so little in it—a threadbare green-sparkle-upholstered couch to the right, a matching chair over at left. The walls were pale yellow swirly plaster, the carpet a urine-yellow shag, and the thought of what might be hiding down in there was a little chilling.

By the row of four front windows, Boyd had set up his surveillance. We were lucky the windows weren't boarded up, though two of them were broken, the glass held in place by their frames and duct tape; mustard-color curtains had been left behind.

"Also from J.C. Penney," he said, gesturing at the khaki folding camping chair, angled to the edge of the window farthest right. His stakeout post.

He'd also gotten himself a cooler and a small portable television. The portable radio I recognized as one he'd brought from home; it was on an easy listening station, Jack Jones singing, "Wives and Lovers." Also from home were the binoculars, which rested on top of a spread-out newspaper near his chair—he would not set those on that questionable carpet—as did his Smith and Wesson .38 long-barreled Model 29 revolver.

I rarely used a revolver. Boyd preferred them over automatics, because the latter sometimes jammed. That was true, but you can't use a silencer on a revolver. We agreed to disagree.

I pulled the green easy chair over and sat, which put the "easy" part in question. He turned the camp chair toward me and settled into it, crossing his legs. Bing Crosby started singing, "Pennies from Heaven."

I asked, "How long you been here?"

"Three goddamn days." He winced at the world around us. "What is the *smell* in this dump?"

"Cat urine. Ancient cat urine, but unmistakable. Like vintage wine."

"Jesus." He shivered, then gestured generally. "I put those air freshener things around, too, and what good are they doing?"

"Not much. How much good are *you* doing?"

He smirked, shook his head. "Not much more than the air fresheners."

"This our only stakeout site?"

Boyd nodded. "That's the saving grace of this shitty job and this shitty shithole."

"What is?"

His head bobbed toward Highland. "We have one-stop shopping here. This character Climer lives on the top floor of the building across the way, in a kind of penthouse. The magazine offices are on the second floor, and of course the club is on the first."

"You been over there?"

He nodded. "Club floor only. Nicer than the outside looks. Mirrors and leather. No cover charge. Pretty girls. Nice bodies. They strip down all the way. If that's what you're into."

"Well, it kind of is."

He flipped a hand. "Drinks aren't weak, or expensive. There's no hooking on the premises, but the girls and the clientele negotiate on the side. Night I went over there, I saw table dances with as much talking as dancing. Then back here at my post, I observed several of the little dears, after closing, meet the gentlemen out front of the club and go off with 'em."

"You think the club is in on that action?"

The other hand flipped. "Don't know. My guess? The management doesn't discourage the hooking, 'cause it brings in the customers. But they probably don't participate because even in this corrupt town, they might get busted big-time."

"You *assuming* the town's corrupt…or did you see something?"

"Saw something. A couple of plainclothes gendarmes who I took to be vice cops got paid off at the bar. Money passed hands with no effort to conceal."

"Was Climer making the payoff himself?"

"Well, *a* Climer was. Max's first and only cousin, Vernon. He runs the club now that Max has turned editor and publisher. I have the Broker's file for you to go over—Vernon's in it."

I frowned. "Does the Broker think Climer's own cousin took out the contract?"

Under the bushy brush of a mustache, white teeth blossomed. "Why, Quarry, would that *shock* you? He's Max Climer's sole close living relation, no brothers or sisters, and Mommy and Daddy went to heaven when Max was but a teen—seems the family moonshine still exploded."

I gave him half a grin. "You gotta be shitting me."

"Not even a little. Max Climer grew up in a cabin straight out of Dogpatch. The family business was shine. Hell, the Climer boys are *still* selling spirits, aren't they?"

"Yeah, but that's not where their fortune's being made. And

somebody in that organization is smart, because their magazine isn't just another skin rag."

The shaggy eyebrows climbed. "Really? And what separates it from the smutty crowd, would you say?"

"For one thing, it's funny as hell. The cartoons, and even the articles, are really off the wall. That rag tells all kinds of important people to go fuck themselves. And it does it in between split-beaver pics."

The ugly phrase made Boyd shudder. Which of course is why I used it. I have to have some fun out of life.

His chin rose so he could look down his nose at me. "So you read *Climax* for the articles, do you, Quarry? Now I've heard *everything*."

"Why, you ever read the magazine?"

"I don't believe I'm the target audience."

"Well, if you ever cracked a cover, you'd know that hillbilly Hefner over there writes editorials in favor of gay rights, women's liberation, and civil liberties in general. Of course, his idea of striking out against racism is running a pictorial of a big black stud banging a young white chick."

Boyd made a face. "Must you?"

"Racial objections?"

"There's no reason to insult me."

"Anyway," I said, "there are all kinds of people who want to silence a guy like Max Climer. It wouldn't have to be a family member who wants to inherit."

The Broker's manila folder was on the cooler. Boyd nodded toward it. "Why don't you go over the file, and see if you have any questions?"

I sat and read it, sipping a Coke courtesy of Boyd, who had a six-pack in his cooler for me, looking after my needs like the good partner he was.

The cousin was in the file. So was a wife, separated but not yet divorced from Climer. And a current girlfriend who'd been a dancer at the club. Also the daughter of cousin Vernon, who was some kind of women's libber. A few other co-workers. Local civic types who'd spoken out against Climer and *Climax Magazine*. Some religious leaders, a few of them potentially dangerous flakes.

Tossing the folder back on the cooler, I said to Boyd, who'd angled his chair back to the window and was using his binoculars, "How have you proceeded, so far?"

He lowered the binoculars, swung his head toward me. "The usual. Keeping an eye on Climer's comings and goings. He stays pretty much to that three-story castle over there. Goes out for an early supper, five, six o'clock. Country boys don't eat late like city folk, I guess."

"You follow him then?"

Boyd nodded. "Haven't been here long enough to know if he's got a regular schedule in that regard. You know, favorite eating spots he frequents."

Some people established a pattern that way, going to favorite restaurants on the same nights of the week, every week.

"So, then," I said, "you barely got back from Vegas when the Broker got in touch and sent you here."

With a few quick nods, Boyd said, "That's right. A little odd, doing two jobs this close together…but Broker's the boss, and this is paying *very* damn well, don't you think?"

I nodded. I didn't want to go into specifics because I might be getting paid more than Boyd. Previously when the Broker sent me in undercover, he'd rewarded me for it. No need to get Boyd's nose out of joint over that.

I said, "You've been following our regular routine?"

"Right."

"As if Climer himself were the target."

"Uh, yes, of course."

I held up a "stop" palm. "Okay, now meaning no offense...*he's* not our target. We have multiple targets here, but Climer is not one of them."

Boyd frowned. He clearly hadn't thought this through. We had our usual way of doing things, and he'd fallen into step. Nor had the Broker thought to give him new directions in this different circumstance.

I said, "Our targets are as follows—first, the team that somebody's sending in to kill Max Climer. Second, whoever hired that team...who we have to identify and then dispatch. Because if we don't, another team will be sent in, and on and on it goes."

Boyd was still frowning. Defensively, he said, "Well, if we keep an eye on Climer, surely that will lead us to—"

"No," I said, cutting him off. "You're assuming if we spot somebody going after the guy...either in that building across the street, or by way of a drive-by kill outside his favorite barbecue joint or something...that we can interrupt things in a timely enough fashion to save his ass and take down the hitters."

And by "we" I really meant "me," because I was the active half here.

"I see your point," he said, and the defensiveness was gone. "And you're right. Sorry. I guess I...I guess I really screwed up."

I waved it off. "Climer isn't dead yet, so forget it. You've picked up worthwhile intel, which is good, but now we have to shift our focus from Climer to the team sent in to take him out."

Boyd sighed, nodded. "Might not be a team, though. Might be a lone wolf. Not everybody works this game the way the Broker does."

"True. But a lot do. Either way, we need to locate the competition and put them out of business…like that café below us."

He smiled, a little embarrassment in it. "Wish a café were down there now. Would come in handy."

"Actually, it wasn't bad."

The shaggy eyebrows came together. "You ate there? When in hell?"

"One of my first jobs for Broker, before he teamed us up, was here in Memphis. They served sandwiches and cold beer and if you used the head, you got yourself a free contact high. It was all hippies and dope back then."

He smirked. "Now it's pussy and pornography."

"Well, not entirely. Seems like this neighborhood is trying to come back to respectable life, and I'm sure Max Climer's presence here is not a happy thing for many of his neighbors."

Boyd frowned. "Unhappy enough to want him dead?"

I grunted a laugh. "Wouldn't surprise me." I stood. "Look, stay at your post. I'm going to take a look around the neighborhood. See I can spot anything or anybody."

Boyd nodded. "Okay. Do that. Good idea. Good thinking. Uh, Quarry?"

I was halfway across the room, heading for the hallway. I glanced back. "Yeah?"

"Sorry I…kind of screwed up."

"Naw, you didn't. We're just getting started here."

"You won't, uh…mention how boneheaded I was to the Broker or anything…?"

"Hell no. And you weren't. Cool it. I'll be back in an hour or two."

Soon I was down on the street where dusk was darkening to night and the air had turned cool even as it stayed dry. I had the black windbreaker on, the nine millimeter (minus the silencer) stuffed in my back waistband—the jacket came down over my hips enough to help hide the weapon.

I took a nice casual walk along both sides of the streets adjacent to the Climax Club. What I was looking for was somebody (or somebodies) sitting in a car without the engine running. Probably a man or men, but a female gun wasn't out of the question—I knew of several who worked for the Broker. In many cases, someone sitting surveillance would tuck into the backseat, keeping down, so that at first glance the car would appear unoccupied.

For now, anyway, I spotted no one who might be on stakeout. But I'd have to stay on top of the possibility.

As I walked, I also looked at the second- and third-floor apartments of buildings close enough to Climer's to provide decent surveillance. On the cross street, the side of the three-story building opposite the front of the club had second-floor lights on above a pawnshop.

The door to the stairs up to the apartment was on Highland, between the pawnshop and a secondhand furniture store. It was unlocked and, after switching on a light inside the door, I went on up to the landing. These stairs were carpeted and not at all creaky, the walls fairly freshly painted, and the door on the landing had also been painted this decade, a friendly bright yellow.

My right hand on my hip, for easy access to the nine millimeter, I knocked with my left. One more knock, and the door cracked open, a young woman with dark curly hair and big brown eyes gazing across the night latch. She was in navy slacks and a navy-and-white polka-dot top, and looked nice if a little harried. The sound of a toddler making a noise that was identifiable neither as happy nor sad was making her wince a little.

"Yes?" she said, talking over the kid noise.

"Oh," I said, "I'm sorry—I thought this was the Lindel residence. Sorry."

I backed away, smiling embarrassedly, and she found a smile and a nod, then closed the door on me.

That was not a lady hitman. Nor was her toddler, though he or she might having been killing mommy by inches.

I went up the remaining flight and knocked several times at a bright green door. No response. Some landlord had spruced the building up, but apparently this apartment was either unoccupied or its renter wasn't home.

I returned to the second-floor landing and knocked again.

As before, the young woman in navy blue answered, frowning over the latch chain, and I said, "Forgive me—this is the last time I'll bother you. But do the Lindels have the upstairs apartment? No one responded to my knock."

"That's because no one lives up there," she said with a painfully forced smile. "If you'll excuse me?"

The door closed a little harder that time. Didn't blame her.

This made the upstairs apartment problematic. If it sat empty, that meant sometime in the next few days it could be occupied by people in the same profession as Boyd and me. It might be occupied by suchlike right now, if those doing so were being discreet and quiet about it.

No other lights were on in nearby second- and third-floor windows. And I knew how to spot minimal light from between windows and curtains, as well as the glint of binoculars.

Nothing.

I returned to Boyd, who was still in his camp chair with his own binoculars at the ready.

Plopping down in the uneasy chair, I said, "I don't think they're here yet. Nobody's running a parked-car stakeout, and I don't see anything suspicious in the rooms with a view."

"Well," Boyd said, brow furrowed, "the Broker indicated he turned this job down only recently. The client would have to find a new broker and things'd have to be set in motion. Could be we're ahead of the curve."

"If we are," I said, "it's just barely. But still an advantage. You had any sleep lately?"

"Some," he said. "According to the advance intel the Broker gave me, Climer sleeps in till noon. Likes to work all night or party the same, depending on his mood and the needs of his magazine. So I've been sleeping in myself. But this has been fucking drudgery, and we're just getting started."

I pawed the air. "Catch yourself some zee's. I'll cover the night shift."

"Cool. I appreciate it, Quarry."

"Don't freak out if I'm not here. I'm going to check out the Climax Club at some point this evening."

"Okay. Don't do anything I wouldn't do."

He'd said this to me before and knew what my response would be.

I gave it to him anyway, with a smile: "No promises on that score."

FOUR

I was a little uptight about Boyd's failure to grasp the different demands of this assignment. I blamed the Broker in part, for not properly prepping him. But maybe my passive half was still off his feed following his break-up with that hairdresser back east. Boyd had been fine on the Vegas job, but on the one before that had damn near got me killed, after he picked up some guy in a bar when he was supposed to be watching my back.

In the coolness of late evening, I stood in front of our boarded-up storefront and looked across the street, surveying the three-story building whose bottom floor was the Climax Club. The first floor had a few bikers and blue-collar types milling around outside, smoking and shooting the shit, while patrons came in and out of the bar. Lively but not crazy—probably a typical weeknight here. The second floor, the *Climax Magazine* offices, was almost dark, some subdued lighting but no sign of activity. The third floor had lights on behind several windows—the penthouse living quarters. It would appear the master of the house was home.

Since I wasn't on the prowl at the moment for a rival team of killers, I'd left the nine millimeter Browning in my room at the stakeout. That was a tricky call, since the job this time hinged on locating targets rather than being pointed to one; but going into the Climax Club with an automatic in my back waistband could be troublesome. Brushing up against the wrong person who recognized the feel of such steel could get me looked at the wrong way.

But with what I had in mind, I couldn't go over there naked.

In anticipation of such a situation, I had bought (back at a Lake Geneva sporting goods shop) a little pocket gun, a walnut-grip Colt .25 with a six-shot clip. This I dropped into my right-hand windbreaker pocket, the jacket's pockets deeper than usual for a garment like that. The little piece would not slip out and go clunking to the floor when I sat down or shifted around or something.

I was at an age now where I didn't often get taken for a college kid anymore, but what the hell—maybe I was a grad student. At any rate, as I entered the Climax Club, I was just a shortish-haired guy in a t-shirt, windbreaker and jeans. Some kind of working stiff. Nicely anonymous. About as suspicious in a joint like this as whoever was sitting next to you at the bar.

But the bar was not where I deposited myself. I took one of the many round tables facing the stage, so I could get a feel for the place. Took a while for my eyes to get used to the cigarette smoke, which was no thicker than if a bonfire had been going.

A stacked redheaded waitress in a green bikini came over and took my order for a Coors, which was on tap; she was cute and friendly with freckles everywhere and frizzed hair like she'd been pleasantly electrocuted. No Bunny outfits in the Climax, no set costume beyond every waitress wearing a bikini and strappy sandals and looking good in one.

The bikinis were about the most distinctive thing about the joint. The only hint that this was the birthplace of a controversial and successful new nationally distributed magazine was an array of framed *Climax* centerfolds that were spotted around the brick walls like a museum devoted to labia. I guess the pink curtains on the windows might be suggestive of what made the mag so popular, too, but that would have required some rather deep and metaphorical thinking from the working stiffs (get it?) in attendance.

Otherwise, the Climax was fairly standard strip club fare—hanging pseudo-Tiffany shades over the pool tables off to the left, a central stage with silver tinsel curtain and a runway along which was the prime seating for those who wanted a good look at where babies come from. To give you the idea of the sleaze level, just as my Coors arrived, a long-legged dark-tanned brunette with fake boobs came strutting out on the stage wearing a red bikini, which was the *start* of her strip act. Waitresses were renting coal-miner helmets for ten bucks a pop to guys seated along the runway, the lights on the helmets bringing the miracle of life into brighter focus, when a dancer crouched before them in pursuit of crumpled cash.

This was a mixed crowd—not racially, as I didn't spot a single black face other than a bartender and a waitress; but in social class, white- and blue-collar, longhairs in jean jackets, a few bikers at the bar, group of Marines in uniform at the little round tables. The music was loud, the DJ in the front right corner keeping things light, cracking jokes ("Make Ginger feel at home, fellas…it's her first time…tonight"), and the high-ceilinged chamber—not much larger than your average neighborhood bar—was anything but rowdy.

Strip bars where the girls get down to their birthday suits often fall into an almost uncomfortable silence, down under the raucous music, a church-like hush, a collective fugue state. Right now a naked little blonde going by Brandi Wyne (I'd seen her poster on my way in—she was a featured dancer who'd been a centerfold in *Climax*) was doing a backward push-up, feet straddling the edge of the stage, sharing a well-trimmed secret with a coal miner staring at her while pretending to be unimpressed.

Security was present but not obnoxious—half a dozen bouncers were positioned at key spots around the room, black slacks, white dress shirts, black bow ties, a lot of muscle, arms folded genie-like so tight their sleeves might burst, their biker hair ponytailed back, their tiny black eyes missing not much.

I watched the show a while. The girls were good-looking and not scary the way they could be in a strip club this raunchy. There was something good-natured about it all, from the goofy miner's caps (surely a Max Climer idea) to the jokey DJ. And, like the waitresses, the dancers were all smiles, not bored and dead-eyed. That was clearly a house policy, although swimming in dollars and fivers could get a girl in a good mood, I'd bet.

Her set finished, Brandi Wyne—in the blue bikini and a filmy negligee wrap—came over and sat at my table. She had Goldie Hawn's hair but more curves, her heart-shaped face not hard yet with a perfect little nose, big brown eyes with blue eye shadow, and a small, provocative mouth painted glistening pink. She also wore musky, flowery perfume, strong enough to cut through the smoke.

"Having fun yet?" she asked chirpily, quoting Zippy the Pinhead though probably not on purpose. Her pupils were big. Cocaine?

"You're a good dancer," I told her, working to be heard over "Tush" on the sound system.

She *had* been good, keeping time anyway, which when you're face up bouncing on your hands and feet with your legs spread, is a real trick. I'd imagine.

"You from here?" she asked.

"No. Want a beer?"

"We only drink champagne."

"Why don't I just give you five dollars and you buy your own champagne, when you get around to it."

She liked that idea, tucking the five in her bikini bottom.

We talked a while. I was a lingerie salesman, which she

found interesting, and she was a student at the University of Memphis, which was no surprise. I was pretty sure we were both lying.

"You're nice," she said. "You want to do something later? I'm off at midnight."

"Check back with me," I said.

She smiled, squeezed my hand, and vaporized.

I knew, from info I'd been provided, that next to the restrooms was a door that led to the publishing floor. Up there, I knew, another stairway rose to the penthouse. What I wanted to know was how hard—or easy—it would be for someone uninvited to get up there.

A bow-tie bouncer was positioned outside the restroom alcove with his back to the wall. I headed past him to the heads and used the one labeled with a rooster silhouette (the other had a pussycat). Upon emerging, I tried the knob on the door to my right, marked EMPLOYEES ONLY, and found it unlocked.

Could it be that easy?

It was.

Up a narrow flight I was suddenly in a space the size of the club below, illuminated only by a few security lights, but instead of a strip club, this was indeed a place where a magazine might be assembled. The sprawling office area had no cubicles and no sectioned-off smaller offices for managers. This was just a big, formerly empty area where a bunch of people who never put a magazine together before assembled to do so. Untidy desks with typewriters were at skewed angles everywhere, as were light tables and artist work stations. Brick walls wore bulletin boards thick with tacked-up photos and photo proof sheets, and book-filled board-and-block shelving straight out of a dorm room huddled under windows with blinds, not pink curtains—a sea of clutter that spoke of hard, energetic, even desperate work.

The hand on my shoulder made me jump.

I slipped my hand into my right windbreaker pocket, gripped the little gun and spun, ready to use it...

...and there stood Brandi Wyne in her curvy little blue-bikini glory, looking up at me with her big brown eyes and their big black pupils.

"I know what you're up to," she said.

"Do you." Hand in pocket, gun in hand.

Christ, just what I needed. Cornered into killing some dumb chick because I'd been dumb enough to go blundering around like I owned the place, making Boyd look smart in comparison.

"You were scoping things out," she said.

"Was I?"

She nodded and the Goldie Hawn helmet bounced. "Havin' a look around. Seein' if you could find some quiet place for us to have a little fun."

Relief flooded through me, and so did something else.

She took her top off and smiled up at me. She had perfect little perky handfuls that looked up at me, too.

"Would you think me terrible," she asked, "if I asked you to help me out with my...what's it called, paying for class?"

"Tuition," I said. What's it called, paying for ass?

"What I could really use," she said, "is twenty-five dollars for books. Could you help?"

I got three tens out of my wallet. "Buy an extra one," I said, and tucked the folded bills in her bikini bottoms. Along the side, not wanting to be crude.

"Come over here," she said, and took me by the hand, leading me to a brown faux-leather couch under some framed *Climax* covers, a little social area resting on a big tan throw shag carpet, which thankfully did not smell like cat pee.

She stood before me and undid my jeans and tugged them and my shorts down, their contents springing free. Then she gave me a friendly push till I was seated and she knelt before me. She took hold of me in a firm but gentle grasp, then looked up all Orphan Annie and said, "Just so you know—I don't swallow."

I shrugged. "Neither do I."

Dear Letters to Climax,

Then the little dancer began to slide her wet warm mouth up and down my throbbing shaft, slow at first, gradually building, building, enveloping it in her velvety oral embrace until my pubic hairs were tickling her little pink nose, then backing off with a small self-satisfied grin to work my saliva-soaked member with her tiny tight hand until she sent streams of white coating her pink breasts, one drop glistening off a nipple like dew from a morning leaf.

Sincerely,

A loyal reader.

P.S. Fortunately I hadn't had to use my .25 Colt, which I kept my hand around in my windbreaker pocket throughout, in case the bouncer on lookout downstairs was her accomplice. If so, she would barely have started her work when I'd likely have been staring down the barrel of a bigger gun than my Colt, handing over everything else in my wallet and probably my car keys, too.

I sat there breathless for maybe a full minute while she got up, scurried over to an end table where *Climax* magazines were stacked and yanked some Kleenex from a dispenser and cleaned my spunk off her tits, morning dew and all. I bet this was her first time blowing a guy up here. Tonight.

"You're nice," she said, handing me a spare tissue. She tossed hers in a nearby wastebasket.

I stood and pulled up my pants, buckled, zipped, then sat again. "Always happy to support higher education."

That seemed to confuse her momentarily, until she remembered her cover story and giggled. She sat down and I did, too.

"What's your name?" she asked.

"Jack."

"Jack like money?"

"Jack like money."

"You think you might come see me again, Jack?"

"Could be. What's your name?"

"Brandi Wyne."

"No. Your *name*."

"Oh. Wanda Roux. I don't think I look like a Wanda, though, do you?"

"Brandi's better," I agreed. "Thanks, honey."

"Thank *you*, honey."

She patted my knee, then got up and scampered over to the sea of desks, where she'd dropped her bikini top. At the sight of her curvy little fanny and the dimples above, my cock tried to lift its exhausted head, but gave up quick. She put on the top, businesslike now, gave me a sad little smile, then an even sadder little wave, and was gone.

So, now I had an excuse to be up here, at least.

What I didn't know was whether Brandi or Wanda or whoever regularly did this. Was she a hooker who sometimes stripped? Or a stripper who occasionally hooked? Did the other girls bring Johns up here for jack, too, and did the house get a cut?

Or did the bouncer standing watch below have an arrangement with the girls to let them come upstairs and (for a cut) pick up some tuition money? And, if so, was this behind the management's back?

Still sitting there, a little dazed by the unexpected attention, I started shaking my head, telling myself no. No, this wasn't a regular thing for girls at the club. As Boyd had said, based on his surveillance, the dancers would negotiate with guys they approached or did table dances for, and then meet them later for off-the-premises fun and games.

Anyway, I was indeed sitting in the *Climax Magazine* offices, where it was unlikely that Climer and his staff would want people intruding, let alone using their couch and shag throw rug as a mini-bordello.

The bouncer possibility was trickier. If indeed little Brandi had a regular deal with one or more of the musclebound watch-dogs to give her time to do a little business upstairs, then the one on duty right now would start getting suspicious if I didn't show up downstairs within a reasonable amount of time. Like, say, within five minutes of Brandi's exit.

A wall of bulletin boards festooned with page proofs and naked-girl pics hemmed in one side of the stairwell. I posi-tioned myself alongside it, with the .25 out of the windbreaker pocket and in hand, ready should that bouncer emerge on the lookout for the blow-ee now that the blow-er had gone back to her dancing duties.

I waited that way for an hour.

Not really. But the ten minutes felt like an hour. And if after that long, the bouncer hadn't come looking for me, I was home free. My mind played it out—Brandi had spotted me head for the can, maybe thought about joining me there, then saw me come out and cut to my right, which meant I was heading upstairs. She'd gone back to the ladies room, slipping past the none-the-wiser bouncer, and trotted up looking for me.

And found me.

So.

Once again I was alone in the sprawling offices of *Climax*. Kind of an anticlimax, though that was fine with me, consid-ering the possibilities. The .25 in hand now, my next stop would be the doorway to Max Climer's penthouse, which was opposite (and halfway across the room from) where the stairs to this floor came out.

Surely that door would be locked.

My little set of lock picks were in my wallet and waiting for just such a contingency. But the door was not locked, and when you opened it, a light came on to show you the way up a green-carpeted, yellow-walled flight. The only thing missing was elevator music. And an elevator.

I was starting to envy the active-and-passive pair hired to take out this guy, whoever they might be. When had Boyd and I ever had it this easy?

Or was it *too* easy?

Of course, chances were the door up there was locked. And possibly, just by opening that door behind me, I'd already set off an alarm. In which case I would need a healthy line of patter if some armed bodyguard was awaiting me behind that final door. Otherwise I would wind up killing some flunky, and wouldn't *that* be sloppy.

But no bodyguard or anyone else was waiting.

In the glow of a hanging daisy-petal lamp, I found myself in a modern kitchen that was everything the one in the stakeout pad across the street wasn't, starting with gleaming appliances—gold refrigerator, avocado range—surrounded by clashing colors and patterns, the gold-and-green geometric wallpaper offset somewhat by dark wood cabinets.

Signs of life included dirty dishes in the avocado sink and empty beer cans (Bud) on a round orange-topped table with white orange-cushioned chairs made of a substance not known in nature. I guess you sat there drinking orange juice in the morning. Or Bud.

A hallway off the kitchen took me past mostly open doors on

both the left and right. Suddenly, here on the third floor of a building with a strip club two floors below and a magazine office one floor down, I might have been in a well-outfitted suburban home, the kind where a really hip young exec and his bride and his little brood were happily nestled.

Door number one, Monty: left—a wood-paneled den with yet another shag carpet (orange), a wet bar with four stools and, in an echo of the club below, a pool table; but also a wall of shelves with a 25" TV and fancy stereo-and-speaker set-up with several hundred LPs to choose from, and a pair of overstuffed brown-leather easy chairs.

Door number two: right—the master bedroom, avocado walls, yellow-and-green bedspread, Victorian brass bed, oak furnishings, Tiffany style bedside lamp. Arty framed charcoal over the bed—a reclining nude woman, her back to us.

Door number three: left—guest bedroom, French Provincial, blindingly ivory including the shag carpet. Good luck to the cleaning lady. Big framed Toulouse-Lautrec can-can print, on a side wall.

Door number four: right—the only closed one, bleeding light at its bottom edge, the muffled sound of country western also seeping out—Johnny Cash?

Door number five: left—gold-and-black bathroom with a hot tub for two and double sinks, big mirror. Black toilet. Just one. Maybe next time.

Finally the hall emptied out into a good-size living room. Not a formal one, but for entertaining, with another wet bar and leather overstuffed chairs and a low-slung armless couch and plush throw carpets on the wall-to-wall pile, in every shade of brown imaginable. Framed geometric designs broke up the brown-and-tan walls with yellow and purple dabs, and a futuristic monstrosity that I guessed was one of those new projection TVs crouched in a corner like a robot trying to hide from spacemen.

Barely audible from the club two floors down came the raucous rock that Brandi and the rest stripped to, helping pay for all this. Was that the Stones? "Only Rock 'N' Roll"?

With the little .25 in hand, I returned to that closed door and opened it (unlocked of course), shouldering in quick, gun first.

The big modern mahogany desk, its surface piled with paperwork, faced me and so did the man seated behind it.

Most of the space in the room was taken up by the desk, the wall behind the man in the swivel chair given to shelves of books, some erotic knickknacks, and a small stereo system with stacks of cassette tapes nearby. Johnny Cash was indeed singing —"Ring of Fire."

Also on the desktop were a phone, some pens, an ashtray with a cigarette going, a can of Budweiser and a .357 Colt magnum. My host's hands were flat on the desk, very casual, spread apart but not terribly near the gun.

He was medium-sized with just a little heft to him, in his early thirties, his eyes dark blue and wide-set and rarely blinking in a smooth, faintly smiling baby face, his hair black and curly and vaguely Caesar-ish—Julius, not Sid. His shirt was a light pink polo with CLIMAX over the breast pocket.

"Are you here to kill me?" Max Climer asked, calm as pass-the-butter. "Or are you the other one?"

FIVE

"If I were here to kill you," I said, with a little lift of the .25-in-hand, "this conversation would already be over."

The benign baby face formed a faint smile, then he nodded and said, "Please," gesturing to a black-leather button-tufted chair over by a side wall where shelves were given over to neatly arranged stacks of magazines, *Playboy* and *Penthouse* and lesser competitors, but also *Time*, *Newsweek*, *Forbes*, *Business Week*. Lower shelves bore banker's boxes with felt-tip designations: LEGAL, POLITICAL, RACIAL, SEXUAL MORES.

I dragged the chair over—it was heavy—and settled into it.

"There's a name I was told to give you," I said, and gave it to him. What exactly its significance was, the Broker hadn't said. I guessed it was one of Climer's investors. Anyway, he acknowledged it with another nod.

"So, then," he said, his voice mid-range with a Southern drawl but no twang, "you're here to help me."

Johnny Cash was singing "It Ain't Me, Babe." Not loud, but with us in the room.

I set the .25 on the desk. The nearby .357 dwarfed it. "Here to help if I can," I said. "But it's tricky."

He leaned back in his own button-tufted leather chair and folded his hands over his belly, rocking a little. "Tricky how?"

"As you know, a mutual friend, actually mutual business associate, has reason to believe someone wants you dead. I'm here to try to keep you alive."

Amusement tweaked his thin lips. "A lot of folks wouldn't mind seein' me dead. But I'm not sure who might consider that worth spendin' good money on. That's what we're talkin' about here, right? A contract killing?"

"Mr. Climer, this is nothing to take lightly." I gestured around us vaguely. "Let's start with your security in this building."

The unblinking blue eyes were half-lidded, as if he might be on something, but I didn't think he was, not counting Budweiser.

"I have half a dozen boys downstairs, all ex-bikers," he said. "My bartenders are equally adept at defending this fort. They have guns behind the bar and baseball bats, too."

"That'll come in handy," I said, "if you join a softball league. You do realize that my little gun and I just walked up here, armed, and waltzed into your inner sanctum? With no trouble at all. The door downstairs, off the Cocks and Pussycats, was unlocked, and so was every door after that."

The faint smile was still there, but at least it was a little fainter now. He tapped the grip of the .357 lightly with his fore- and middle fingers and said, "Maybe I figure I can take care of myself."

"A gun only works when it's in your hand and you're firing it—that is, firing it *before* the other guy does. If I wasn't on your side? You'd have got a bullet in your head before you opened your mouth."

Some defensiveness came into his tone; barely discernible, but there. "I travel with an armed chauffeur."

"Not in this penthouse you don't. Can we agree your in-house security needs work? By which I mean, it sucks?"

"You have a point," he conceded.

"Yale locks on every one of those doors would be a start. Anybody worth half a shit could open one with two picks, but using 'em on that door down in the club, out in the open, would be a good fucking trick."

He nodded.

"You need an alarm system."

"There's one in the club."

"How about this floor? And the magazine office?"

His grin was a lazy thing that told me I'd sold him; whatever I suggested, he'd do.

"You want a beer?" he asked. "Got a name, by the way?"

"I'd take a beer if it's not Bud. Got a Coors? Call me Quarry."

He frowned at me, rising. "You don't really drink *Coors*, do you? It's like makin' love in a boat—fuckin' close to water! All I got's Budweiser."

"Got any Coke?"

"Wanna do lines or you mean the sugar shit?" He laughed, as he came out from around the desk, leaving the .357 behind. "Just funnin' ya. And it's Max, by the way. We don't stand on ceremony around here."

Just as Johnny Cash was starting to sing "The Rebel" from the old Johnny Yuma TV show, I slipped the .25 in the wind-breaker jacket pocket and followed him back to the kitchen. He got himself a can of Bud and me a can of Coke, and then said, "You play pool?"

"Been known to."

Climer led me into the wood-paneled den. He was in jeans and bare feet, and maybe an inch shorter than me—of course, I was in shoes. He went over to the stereo set-up and wall of LPs and said, "So you drink Coors. What do you listen to? The Lennon Sisters?"

I had to smile. "If it has to be country western, stick with Johnny Cash or Patsy Cline. Otherwise I might kill you myself."

That got a chuckle out of him. "We'll make it soul. How about Otis Redding? You're in Memphis. Listenin' to Otis is practically the law down here."

"Wouldn't want to do anything illegal."

He put on *Otis Blue*. Again, not loud—just a presence.

We played eightball. He broke, sinking three balls, then ran the table. No conversation, just pool, with "Shake" getting some additional (if out-of-rhythm) percussion by way of the clack-clack of the balls.

"Glad it's not for money," I said.

He chalked his cue. "Now you."

I broke, sinking two balls, then ran the table.

He stared at the green felt where only the cue ball lived now. "Who's the hustler here, I wonder?"

He broke again, but this time the eight ball found a pocket, and he lost interest, saying, "Best two out of three means it's yours. Don't you wish we were playin' for money?"

My host got himself another Bud, this time a bottle from a refrigerator behind the bar—I'd finished the Coke and didn't want another. He gestured in the casual way a pasha might toward the two big comfy-looking leather chairs angled toward the wall of LPs and the stereo set-up. Otis was singing "Wonderful World."

"So," he said, "Yale locks."

"Like I said, just a start. Those ex-bikers, any more of them available?"

He nodded. "I can put together a small army of hard-asses. Guns, chains, knives."

"Well, army might be the operative term. Any of these biker types ex-military?"

"Some."

"Use those."

The dark-blue eyes were only a third lidded now. "I was told *you* were ex-military," he said, and sipped the Bud.

"That's right."

"Silver Star?"

"Bronze actually."

"You saw action?"

"I did."

"Rank?"

"Corporal."

"What exactly did you do over there?"

"Sniper."

"So, then…killing people is not, uh, a problem."

"Well, it is for them."

He thought about that. A low-slung glass coffee table held a couple of glass Climax Club ashtrays, clean, a silver naked-girl lighter, and a pack of Camels. He shook out a smoke, lighted it with the naked girl, offered the pack to me, and I declined.

"What branch, Quarry?"

"Marines."

"I was in the navy. Between wars. Loved it. I made a lot of money off those hick kids from Bum Fuck, Idaho, and Loose Goose, Montana. Poker, on the ship. And pool, on shore leave."

"But you didn't stay in?"

He gulped more Bud. "No. Too damn dull, long run. I was born to the damn bar business. Sold moonshine for my old man, then after the navy, I bought government booze and sold it in dry states. Lived with my aunt and uncle, and they had a bar here in Memphis. Bought 'em out and the rest is history. So what's your story?"

He seemed to want to know.

"Took what skills I picked up in the Marines," I said, "into private industry."

That could hardly have been more sketchy, but it satisfied him.

"Security," he said, interpreting it his own way. "And now you're here to help me. As a high-end bodyguard?"

"Not exactly…"

"Till this scare is over," he said, ignoring that, cigarette between two fingers of the hand he was gesturing with, "you'll be at my side, running the show with the extra boys I put on."

I raised a "stop" palm. "No, Max, I may be serving that function from time to time, but I have a bigger job."

A rare blink. "What job's bigger than protecting my ass?"

"I know how to spot the kind of people who've been sent to take you out. And I also hope to figure out who might have hired this thing in the first place."

Climer thought about that while Otis did his blistering "Satisfaction." Then he said, softly, "If you pinpoint the assassin…"

"Likely a team of two. Yes. Go on."

"If you spot these people, Quarry, what will you do?"

"Do you want to know?"

"Do I?"

"I would say…no. But keep in mind, if I remove those sent to take you out, that doesn't solve the larger problem. Another pair would be fast on their heels. There's only one way to really stop this. We need to look at who might've hired them."

His frown barely registered on the childish face. "Christ. That could be anybody from half a dozen screwball religious groups…we're not talking Presbyterians, but cult kooks who handle snakes and talk in tongues…to the Highland Strip Merchants Association, who think the Climax Club and my publication bring down the moral tone of Memphis in general and their precious little strip of it in particular."

I shrugged. "It's probably *not* a group, unless you've tangled personally with a strong leader who considers you a personal enemy. Of course, you *have* been known to inject yourself into controversy. To encourage readers and the public at large to see your magazine as an extension of Max Climer, and vice versa."

The faint smile returned. "You almost sound like a reader yourself."

"I am one. Hell, I'm a subscriber."

Now the smile flashed some small, rather feral teeth. "You *are* a loyal reader!"

"I am. Or maybe I just don't want to be embarrassed buying that rag of yours in public."

That made him laugh. He laughed a while, actually, with Otis singing "You Don't Miss Your Water" in the background.

When the album was over, Climer got up, dirtied one of the ashtrays stubbing out the Camel, flipped the disc on the turntable, and Otis started in on "Ole Man Trouble."

As he settled back in the comfy chair, I said, "Tell me about the people in your life."

He frowned again, really frowned, the first time I'd seen him seriously wrinkle that baby face, or anyway the forehead part of it.

"I am surrounded by people who love me, and I love them," he said, the defensiveness back. "I really can't see you wastin' your time going down that road."

"People rarely get killed by people they don't know," I said. "It's usually a relative or close friend."

"A hired killer is a stranger to the victim," he said.

"Right. Hired to do it by somebody the victim knows, or maybe loves. Do you live here alone?"

He shook his head. "No, my fiancée lives with me."

"Where is she now?"

"Downstairs. In the club."

"Why?"

He lighted up a fresh Camel with the naked-girl lighter.

"She's one of the dancers. That's how we met. I cast all of the dancers myself, just like I pick the centerfolds."

"She *still* dances? Engaged to the boss?"

He nodded, shrugged. "Likes to keep her hand in."

I didn't figure her hand was what she was keeping in, but I let it go.

"What's her name?"

"Mavis Crosby. That's her *real* name, doesn't use a stage name, which is rare. She's from around here, like I am. Brimming with ideas for the magazine. Country girl but you'd never know it. She just oozes sophistication."

Something about that didn't sound so appealing.

I asked, "You two get along? No fights? No arguments?"

He smirked, let smoke out his nostrils. "Well...every couple has those. But I don't hit her. I tried that once and she let me know I wouldn't try it again else she'd kill me."

He hadn't even noticed what he said.

"She was abused as a kid," he went on. "Her father banged her ten ways to Sunday and her momma didn't give two shits about it. Of course, that's true of most strippers and pretty much all hookers."

"You plan to have her sign a pre-nup?"

His head reared back, as if ducking a punch. "Hell no! I love her."

"What happened to Dorrie?"

His eyes widened. "How...how do you know Dorrie?"

"I'm a *Climax* reader, remember? You met her in junior high, both thirteen when you first made it, in a hayloft—classic. The star-crossed romance fell apart when you dropped out of the seventh grade to travel with a carnival. Ran the Tilt-a-Whirl, right? Got together years later, childhood sweethearts who got married, and then you did that photo layout of her, in an early issue?"

"Oh, yeah." He almost seemed embarrassed, but also a little impressed by this loyal reader's recall. "Well, see, I published a letter from a guy pissed off because his honey posed nude for us—he wanted to know how *I'd* like it if *my* girlfriend or wife posed bare-ass naked in some grotty magazine for other guys to jerk off to. So I had Dorrie pose so I could say, well, I like it just fine! Jerk away! But that…that's only *part* of the truth."

"What's the rest?"

He lifted a shoulder and put it down. "I didn't have to pay Dorrie for posin', and those were early days. She was fine-looking and didn't mind showing it all to the world. Said that someday she'd be happy she had photos of herself when her boobs were perky and her ass was tight. She's a great gal, Dorrie."

"But you broke up anyway."

He nodded, sighed smoke. "Dorrie couldn't handle my appetites. I don't believe monogamy is a natural state for the male of the species. I have too many opportunities and I don't feel like turnin' 'em down."

"But aren't you planning to marry, what's her name…?"

His grin for the first time revealed a lascivious streak. "Mavis. Yes. Mav doesn't believe in monogamy either, and likes makin' it with other ladies, which doesn't bother me one little bit. Sometimes I just watch, other times I join in."

"Where does this leave Dorrie? Out in the cold?"

His palms pawed the air. "Oh no, no way, not at all. We're getting a divorce and Dorrie will be well taken care of. She be swimmin' in alimony, and that's how I want it. We didn't have kids, so no child support. But a great settlement. Hey, we're still friends. We just grew apart, and it wasn't just my more forward sexual attitudes. See…she married me when I was just this sleazy guy runnin' strip clubs, and then when we started the magazine, and it really took off, she didn't keep up. Maybe *couldn't* keep up."

"Keep up with what?"

He spread his arms and turned up his hands. "With *me*, I guess. I'm a *reader* now. You saw those books in my study! I know more about the law than most lawyers—I *have* to, with all the legal battles I'm fighting. I'm practically a goddamn constitutional scholar, when it comes to the First Amendment. I'm starting to be known as a battler for Civil Rights, and that's really big for a backwoods Southern boy, bein' all for the gays and all for the blacks. *You're* a *Climax* subscriber. Do you read my editorials, or are you just there for the pussy?"

"I take it all in, Max, including 'Dickhead of the Month'— Gerald Ford, last time, right? But how does Dorrie feel about being left behind in a cloud of social commentary?"

He waved that off. "I *told* you, man. We're friends. We'll *always* be tight. And she's been well taken care of. Talk to her and see!"

"I plan to. I may need your help coming up with an excuse to bother her…but I plan to. Who else is in your inner circle?"

I had all that intel from Broker on key figures, photos included, but I wanted to hear it from Climer.

He gulped some more Bud. "Well, cousin Vernon, of course. He's Vice President of Climax Enterprises. Mostly he runs the clubs, but he's involved with the magazine, too. In the early days he dealt with both the printer and distributors. Still handles the latter."

"You're friendly?"

"Tight! Like brothers. We grew up together. And don't forget, I made him rich. Who doesn't love somebody who made 'em rich?"

And who didn't resent somebody who made them rich?

I asked, "How did you come to grow up with Vernon?"

"My folks were in the moonshine business in the hills. A still blew them to high Heaven or maybe Hell. I was, oh, thirteen. Vernon's mama and papa, my aunt and uncle, took me in. I told you, my aunt owned a bar and, after the navy, I bought her out and that's where it all started."

"How did you wind up publishing a magazine?"

Another shrug. "Well, at first it was just a newsletter with nude pics of the dancers, saying which club they'd be at. To stay legal, we added more copy, little articles about the girls. And then the newsletter turned into a little slick flier, and then that became a magazine. I got some investors together and put the rest of the first issue on my credit card and Vernon's, and we sold fifty thousand copies out of the gate. Rest is history."

"No other business partners you haven't mentioned?"

"No. Just Vernon and me. And he still owns a third of Climax Enterprises, ink."

"No mob money?"

"Hell no! I wouldn't touch it."

"I need to know, Max. Mobsters love to invest in porn."

"Not *my* porn!"

But the Broker was an investor—did Climer really not know the nature of some of the money that got him off the ground?

I asked him about the staff of the magazine, looking for Broker's quisling, but Climer insisted they were all longtime friends from his club business who, like him, had learned how to put a publication together by trial and error. No one had been fired from this inner circle, and no one currently appeared disgruntled. Beyond that, *Climax Magazine* was a huge success that they'd been in on the ground floor of, and none of them had any reason to bitch, much less want the Big Daddy responsible to get dead.

"Let's go back to those civic groups and religious fanatics," I said. "Are there any leaders who might have a real grudge? Someone you've badly embarrassed in public, maybe? Or somebody so crazed he or she might take you for the devil incarnate?"

Otis started in on "Change Gonna Come" while my host reflected.

"There's Lesser Weaver," he said, stubbing the second cigarette in the tray. "He's a wild-eyed fanatic with a fervent following. His Evangelical Redeemer Church stages protests outside the club maybe once a month, more lately. But I think Weaver has another agenda than doing the Lord's work."

"What would that be?"

The faint smile made a comeback. "He knows I'm moving to Germantown."

"Moving where?"

"It's a very well-off, very white conservative suburb with a crime rate lower than a rat's nuts. And the idea of me moving in is driving a lot of them upper-class types bug-fuck."

"You're setting up shop there?"

"No! I'm buying a house. A mansion, actually. I have to do *something* with all this money."

I gestured around us. "What about all this?"

"It's been nice. But I'm tired of living where I work, and this apartment will make a lucrative piece of real estate. No, I'm ready for more, a really fancy layout. Anyway, Mavis is a class act and she deserves the best."

Mavis, of course, was downstairs doing her class act, if by class act you meant letting guys in miner's helmets point their lamps at your privates.

"You know, Max," I said, "it's fun sticking it to people who think they're better than you are…"

"Stickin' it right in their fuckin' *faces*!"

"…but why borrow trouble? Set your business up in a part of town where you're appreciated. Buy a home somewhere they're glad to have you. You're a smut peddler, my friend, not an agent of social change."

"Why not be both, Quarry? Another Coke?"

SIX

Climer and I decided something approaching the outskirts of the real situation would make the best pretext for my presence in his world.

At ten the next morning, he assembled the staff of his magazine around a conference table off to one side of the big cluttered work area. The employees were an even mix of male and female with the long-haired look of mildly reformed hippies. They were all in t-shirts and jeans, with only two exceptions: Climer in a big-collar blue paisley shirt with a gold chain and dollar-sign symbol; and his cousin Vernon, in a vested light-tan wide-lapel polyester suit with leather buttons and big-collar white shirt, no tie. Vernon looked like he couldn't decide whether he was going to a boardroom or a disco.

Climer's cousin was taller than the baby-faced Caesar at the head of the conference table, probably topping six foot, but was so thin he seemed taller yet. He was maybe forty, his face long and lean and sharp-chinned, with sky-blue eyes behind big tortoiseshell-framed glasses. Sunken cheeks made his cheekbones look even more prominent, his hair sandy and thinning, though some skill had been applied to make it seem less so, his too-dark mustache apparently on loan from Harry Reems.

I was not seated at the table, where the positioning of staffers was already set. Climer provided me with a chair just behind him and to his right, a few feet away. After some conversation among little groups within the group, and the fetching of coffee and lighting of cigarettes, the editor and publisher of *Climax Magazine* lifted a benedictory hand and introduced me.

As I stood, nodding to them like the new kid in class, Climer said, "This is Jack Quarry. He's our new security consultant."

Heads bobbed my way, with expressions ranging from skeptical to confused, from interested to don't-give-a-shit, and I nodded again and sat.

"I brought Jack in," Climer said, "because I noticed we've gotten a little sloppy in the security department, and with all these protests and legal hassles, we really need to batten down the hatches."

Everybody nodded at that.

"I know we've all got a lot on our plate," Climer said, "with deadline coming up, so we'll just get a little report from Vernon on distribution, and then see if anybody has anything else the group needs to address…and then get off our fuckin' asses and go entertain America in the most tasteless way possible."

That got smiles and grins and one "Fuckin' A," but it was clear the enthusiasm level was tamped down by a demanding workload. This was a small group to be putting out a magazine with the success and circulation of *Climax*. I was witnessing growing pains in real time.

Vernon cast smiles at everyone and got perfunctory ones back from those who bothered. In a similar mid-range voice to his cousin, absent the drawl—he'd worked hard to lose it, I'd wager—the V.P. of Climax Enterprises reported an increased circulation of the magazine, "thanks largely to those nude paparazzi photos of Florence Henderson last issue." This perked the table up to the tune of some applause and even some hoots and hollers.

The meeting that followed was brief and dealt with ongoing exploration of expansion into XXX-video production and spin-off magazines, which I zoned out on while I studied the various faces at the table. These loyal if harried staffers did not seem likely candidates for paying to have their boss killed. Surely they wanted him dead from time to time, like all employees do their employers, but that was hypothetical homicide and anyway they couldn't afford it.

So I didn't bother getting their names straight and had no intention of talking to any of them.

The exception, of course, was Vernon Climer, who as he rose from the table and headed away, I intercepted with an arm on his sleeve.

"Mr. Climer, could I have a few minutes?"

He froze and glanced back, as if this were a game of tag. His smile had the kind of rehearsed look behind which unsmiling thoughts lurk.

"I am a tad busy," he said.

Neither of us realized how nearby Max Climer was, so we were both startled a bit when his hands were on our respective nearby shoulders.

"Now, Cousin," Climer said, with his thin-lipped, teeth-stingy smile, "I need you to cooperate with my friend Jack, here. Eminently qualified individual. He's the little brother of an old navy pal of mine."

That was the story we'd settled on.

"Jack here is a Bronze Star winner," Climer said, releasing our shoulders, turning to go, his work done here. "Vietnam vet."

Vernon's smile continued and so did whatever thoughts he wasn't sharing; but he did extend a hand for me to shake, which I did. Clammy.

"Perhaps you would join me in my office, Mr. Quarry?"

"Make it Jack."

"Make it Vernon."

We traded insincere grins.

"I didn't know there were any offices up here," I said, nodding to the cluttered but open space.

"Oh, there aren't any. Max works upstairs in his penthouse hidey hole, then comes down as necessary…or when he feels like checking on the troops. My office is on the first floor."

I followed him down the stairs that opened onto the restroom alcove and then trailed him out into the club. Nothing was sadder or less sexy than a strip club by day during CLOSED hours: the undersides of chairs on tables giving up chewing-gum graveyards, swept-up piles of ashes and worse awaiting further attention, the sickening scent of cheap perfume fighting the heavier smell of smoke while puke stench triumphed, the smears on the runway stage where female bodies had gyrated, their ass smudges like giant thumb prints that weren't in the police files.

The unmanned bar loomed on my left, but Vernon cut sharper left, past the DJ booth, and led me down a small hallway. Behind the stage, a door announced the strippers' collective dressing room (EMPLOYEES ONLY, with *Fuckwad!* added in marker) while one opposite labeled PRIVATE ("Fuckwad!" understood) was obviously Vernon's office.

He opened the door for me to enter. Neither spacious nor cramped, this was as surprising in its way as Climer's penthouse: cherrywood-paneled walls with ebony-framed prints—a Nagel nude, a Lichtenstein pop art panel, a Warhol "Marilyn"; matching mahogany desk, button-tufted black leather chair, captain's chairs for visitors, file cabinets; three-seater chocolate leather couch along one side wall; and well-stocked liquor cart along the other.

I took one of the captain's chairs as Vernon settled behind the big desk, which, like his cousin's, had many piles of papers, if more neatly arranged, as well as a phone and the usual para-phernalia. An antique wooden box revealed itself as a humidor when he opened it and helped himself to a formidable cigar, then offered me one. I declined.

He used a naked-girl lighter, the twin of the one upstairs, to fire up the Cuban, or anyway that's what I bet it was.

"If you'd like a drink," he said, between getting-it-going puffs of the cigar, "help yourself."

The liquor cart was at my left.

"No thanks," I said.

"Hope you don't mind," he said, with a wave of a hand bearing the cigar as well as two gold-nugget rings, "but it's the least of the vices you're likely to run into around here."

The cigar smoke smelled fine. Or maybe it was just better than the cheap perfume/cigarette-smoke/beer-puke bouquet on the other side of the door.

"I appreciate you giving me some time," I said. "Sounds like you have a lot on your hands."

He nodded. "The price of success. Max is a great big kid and talented as hell, a genius in his way. But he's got a tiger by the tail here."

"You mean *Climax Magazine* and its offshoots are expanding exponentially."

His eyebrows lifted above the big-framed glasses. He hadn't expected a five-dollar word from the likes of me. We were even—I hadn't expected an executive office in the back of a strip club.

"That's exactly the problem, so many opportunities," he said, grinning around the cigar. "Though as problems go, it's a sweet one. This club here, it's nothing special, wouldn't you agree?"

I shrugged. "It's all right. If a guy wants a beer and a look at an actual vagina, he could do worse."

He laughed, rested the big smoke in a glass Climax Club

ashtray. "I'm not going to bother remodeling—we'll be putting this building on the market as soon as Max and his girlfriend move out of here."

"Yeah. Movin' on up, like the Jeffersons."

"More like the Beverly Hillbillies," Vernon said, chortling. "Max is buying an honest-to-God mansion over there in Germantown."

"Capone had one. Why shouldn't Max Climer?"

"No argument on that score. Max is like Capone in that he knows what people want. Well, what *men* want, anyway. Some people think it's strictly sex that sells our magazine, but really it's a combination of things—raunchy cartoons like dirty jokes come to life, sex advice, political rants."

"It's a winning cocktail. What were you saying about not remodeling?"

He resumed smoking the cigar, puffed while he spoke, as if a steam engine were fueling his thoughts.

"What Hefner did with the Playboy Clubs, for the white-collar set and wealthy," he said, "we're going to do for the blue-collar crowd and middle-class. Our Climax Lounges will have lots of chrome and shiny surfaces and good-looking waitresses, and we'll keep the stripping aspect, but clean it up some. A real gentleman's club for those who aren't really gentlemen."

"Sounds surefire. This was your cousin's idea?"

He grinned around the cigar again. "Well…as much mine as his. Really, mine. But he's on board, mostly."

"Mostly?"

"I'm still working on the projected financials."

How was that for a vague term that sounded specific?

"And of course," he went on, "the magazine is going great guns. All in under two years. Having nude photos of a former First Lady is what *built* this company, you know."

"The Florence Henderson ones didn't hurt."

"No they didn't. Of course, she's suing us, says they're fakes, but we've got a good case." He sighed cigar smoke. "That's another thing dragging us down—so many legal matters. Lawsuits, obscenity busts…just keeping Max's ass out of jail is a full-time job."

"Well, you have lawyers to do that."

"We do, a local firm, but increasingly they're in over their heads. I have to spend a shitload of time just keeping up with them, not to mention keeping *them* up with *me*….Right now I'm exploring shifting to a firm out of Chicago, used to handling our kind of problems. And that's all tied in with distribution, because often it's our distributors who get hit with local and state obscenity charges, and we try to stand behind them."

"You need a pair of roller skates."

He lifted his shoulders and set them back down. "All part of our growing pains. And Max hates to see this thing get away from us, wants to keep it small…no, not small, but manageable, with a payroll chiefly of friends who've been with us from the start. But it's not manageable, with the scale of what's coming."

"What's coming, besides the clubs you envision?"

He adjusted the big-framed glasses. "Max wants to move into video production—home video is the next big thing, he says—and to create more magazines outside the sex genre. Both ideas I admit I'm not yet keen on, especially since he's reluctant to take on new people. Still, I've learned not to underestimate him. He's a handful, our Max, so much talent and enthusiasm…but he needs a guiding hand."

"Sounds like he's lucky to have you."

A smile blossomed around the cigar. "Kind of you to say, Jack. And I'm pleased that you're on board."

"Really? Why?"

He frowned thoughtfully. "Security really has been terribly lax around here. Having a consultant who can analyze the weaknesses and shore up our defenses is just what we need right now. We've been inundated by protesters, from the religious right to women's libbers, which to a degree is a positive, in that it generates attention. No such thing as bad publicity, as they say. But there are nuts out there who really would like to hang Max Climer on the cross."

"To die for his sins?"

"No, Jack—for their *own* sins. Their own smug satisfaction. Max is the linchpin of our success. Keep him safe, would you?"

"Do my best."

A knock at the door behind me was followed by the caller coming in without waiting to be asked.

I didn't recognize her at first.

She might been one of the strippers, certainly attractive enough, but a shade old and maybe a little heavy for that, her clothes—black blouse with red necklace, red skirt, black wedgies—not slutty enough for a stripper…a housewife out to meet her girlfriends for lunch, maybe. Her straight, shoulder-brushing hair split the difference between brunette and blonde, and her lip gloss was the same bright red as her blouse and skirt, eye shadow light blue, eyes big and brown. Pretty in a harsh way, like Hot Lips on *M*A*S*H*.

Thing was…I'd seen her in the nude. Hell, I'd seen her with her red-nailed fingers spreading open the pink petals between her thighs. And between the staples.

She was Dorrie Climer, and housewife had been right, sort of. She was Max's soon-to-be ex, wasn't she?

"Oh, I'm sorry, Vernon," she said in a voice sultry and lower-pitched than her estranged husband's. "I was just here to, uh, pick up my check."

His mouth smiled, forehead frowned. "Can I drop it by this afternoon, Dorrie? Haven't got to that yet. Uh, this is Jack Quarry, our new security consultant. Jack, this is Dorrie Climer, Max's…"

He didn't quite know how to fill that in.

"I'm a fan," I said and smiled at her, nodding.

She grinned embarrassedly.

"Sorry," she said, and ducked back out.

I got up. "Would you excuse me, Vernon? Anyway, I should let you get back to work."

"Fine," he said, cigar in hand. It needed re-lighting.

I slipped out after her, caught up in the empty club just before she went out the door.

"Excuse me, Mrs. Climer," I said, touching her sleeve. She stopped with a jerk and looked back at me, unsettled.

I removed my hand. "Sorry."

She paused. "What is it you want?"

"I was hoping we might chat for a few minutes."

Her eyes flared, nostrils, too. "Whatever for?"

"I'm just trying to get a sense of this place and what it's about. Your husband's had some death threats and I hoped you might share some insights."

Now the eyes tightened. "Well, I don't know that I want to talk about anything here. I'm not entirely comfortable in this place."

"Okay," I said, and held the door open for her.

She went out, frowning, but more in confusion than anything else.

It was humid but not hot—a pleasant oven that wasn't trying too hard. She looked at me with something approaching suspicion, or anyway wanting to know why she should be giving me any time at all.

"Could I buy you a cup of coffee?" I asked. "Or maybe a late breakfast or early lunch? It's almost eleven."

She studied me, took in air, let out air. "Are you on my husband's expense account?"

I was on the Broker's expense account, but I knew the answer she wanted.

"Yes," I said.

"Then I'll let you buy me lunch. Mr. Quarry, is it?"

"Jack."

She nodded up the street. "Anderton's isn't far."

Small talk accompanied the ten-minute walk through the not-busy shopping district. I told her I was from Ohio, which I used to be, and that I was the brother of a navy friend of Max's, and so on. A Vietnam vet doing security work.

"Are you Max's bodyguard?"

"Not permanently. I'll only be here a few weeks." Actually, I doubted I'd be here anywhere near that long. "And only when he's making a public appearance."

"Otherwise you're consulting."

"Yes."

"About security."

"Right."

"And what does a security consultant do? And if you say, consult about security, I won't let you buy me lunch."

I risked a boyish smile. "You mean if I say I consult about security, you'll buy *me* lunch?"

That got a light chuckle out of her. Nice and kind of throaty.

Anderton's had a nautical theme and was in part an oyster bar. We sat across from each other in a two-tone green booth by a sea-foam-color wall with a swordfish flying on it. She ordered fish and chips and so did I. When in Rome.

We had iced tea. I remembered to ask for it unsweetened. There was bread to nibble.

She asked, "What can I tell you about my husband?"

"Are you as friendly as he says you are?"

"You mean, am I a friendly person, or are Max and I still friendly?"

"I already know you're a friendly person."

"No you don't. I've actually been a little cold."

"You mean a little cold during your lifetime or just to me right today?"

That made her chuckle again. The old Quarry charm was working its magic.

"I get along with Max okay," she said unconvincingly. "I've resigned myself to reality."

"What is reality?"

"That's a wonderful and deep question."

"Give me the shallow answer."

"…The shallow answer is, he likes to fuck other women. Oh, he still liked to fuck me at times. But mostly the girls at his club and ones who posed for him and now this witch he's living with."

"*You* posed for him."

"Yes I did. Why? Did you see it?"

"I saw it. I wasn't lying when I said I was a fan."

"And what do you think?"

"I think your husband is out of his mind."

Her smile burned red. "Very kind of you to say. Of course, Max *is* out of his mind, in a way that has turned out to be very profitable. And he's not ungenerous. I was picking up my monthly check, earlier, when you and I ran into each other. And the settlement we're working out seems generous to a fault."

"I have a suggestion."

"You do?"

"Ask for that penthouse pad of his. If Vernon Climer's to be believed, that club will be gone soon and so will the magazine offices, and it's quite a place, that upstairs. Just have him throw it in."

Her lips pursed in a nice plump smile. "That's a good piece of advice. I hadn't thought of that. Probably the thought of him and that silicone sweetie of his fucking and sucking their way from room to room, well, probably made me too sick to consider it. But it's a good idea. Fine idea. Do you really think Max is in danger?"

I sipped unsweetened iced tea. "Well, it's hard to say. He stirs up a lot of controversy, both locally and nationally. I don't have to tell you, there've been a lot of protests. Do you think there's anybody in particular who might really have it in for him?"

"Like do-him-harm have it in for him?"

"Right. More than just wave signs and yell outside his place of business."

"Maybe. That insane preacher, possibly. That creep who chairs the Highland Strip organization, merchants whatever, he's a hypocrite and a half."

"How so?"

"He owns two porno bookshops in other parts of town."

"Ah. People who live in glass houses…"

"Should keep their fucking trousers on."

Our food came. Very good, great batter on the cod, not greasy; real hand-cut fries. My fountain Coke was just the right mix of syrup and soda water. I was having a fine time.

We returned to small talk for the meal. I asked her where she was living and she said an apartment in the better part of downtown. She liked being close to the restaurants and the music, but the tourists sometimes got her down. Was she working? No, she was happy to live off Max Climer's money. She had worked hard to help him become the publishing magnate of today, and had no problem spending the rest of her life living off him.

When our dishes had been cleared, we lingered for coffee and another iced tea.

"So," she said, "you, uh…liked what you saw."

"Pardon?"

"In *Climax*. Of me."

"Oh. Yes."

"Did you ever…you know."

"Get out the hand lotion in your honor?"

She blushed. Actually fucking blushed. "You're making fun of me."

"Not at all."

"I'm about ten pounds heavier now."

More like fifteen.

I said, "Looks great on you."

"How can you tell?"

"I can tell."

"Not really, though. Did you know the Holiday Inn chain is based in Memphis?"

"No I didn't."

"Do you know what's a few blocks from here?"

"No."

"One of the first Holiday Inns anywhere. It's historic. Pay for lunch, and I'll take you over there and give you a tour."

She *was* a little heavier, but it was fine by me. Her breasts were breathtakingly full, her rib cage sweeping to a narrow waist, her ass two lush handfuls. She must have had access to a pool somewhere because she had a bikini tan that served to make the dark tips and only slightly darker areolae stand out on the pale mounds and the jungle growth of her loins scream against the surrounding white. She lay naked on the bed in the nothing room and propped a pillow under her. I was getting out of my clothes like I was trying to break a record.

"Don't use anything," she said in her throaty way. "I'm on the pill and I've been wasting it. Nobody's had me for months. Are you clean?"

"As a whistle."

"Good. Then just stick it in me. I'll show you where."

She parted her pussy lips just like in the magazine.

Was it unethical, I wondered, fucking Max Climer's wife or whatever him dumping her made her? Hell, the way I saw it, I was helping her self-esteem.

And me screwing her wasn't going to kill him.

SEVEN

For the next two days, Boyd and I shared walking the immediate area around the Climax Club, looking for signs of surveillance either by parked car or apartment. He took days while I took evenings, though some of my time was spent inside the club, where Climer had introduced me around to bartenders, bouncers and waitresses as a security guy who was to be cooperated with, and comped on drinks.

The head bartender, Leon, was the only black guy on staff, big, broad-shouldered, with a shaved head and an easy, broad grin. His manner was friendly but something about his eyes wasn't.

That first evening Climer—who rarely came down to the club—went out of his way to introduce me only to one of the strippers...not surprisingly, his fiancée Mavis, who turned out to be the lanky fake-boobs brunette I'd seen dancing the night before.

We sat at a small round table, the three of us, with her in the red bikini and a sheer red lingerie item that hid as much of her as Saran Wrap does a sandwich. She had the high, prominent cheekbones of a fashion model, only her face had a long, horsey look. Her eyes were big and dark brown in their light-brown eye-shadow setting, living a little too close to her long narrow nose; they were also sleepy.

For somebody who insisted on continuing dancing despite her engagement to her multi-millionaire boss, Mavis Crosby didn't have a whole lot of energy. When she went on, later, her dancing seemed languid, too, though at least she stayed on beat to a selection of tunes ("Lean On Me," "Killing Me Softly") that were perhaps chosen for their dreamily undemanding tempos.

Right now she was listening to Climer, who was saying, "You're going to see a lot of Jack around here, for a while. He's our new security guy."

Mavis tilted her head and narrowed her eyes, looking from Climer to me and back again. "Who was our old one?"

Climer's tiny smile in the rarely blinking baby face only made him seem more childlike. "We never really had one, honey, and that's the problem."

"But what about Freddie and Lou and them?" She meant the half dozen bouncers on staff.

"Well, they do security at the club. But we need *more*—for the magazine, and our pad upstairs, and better locks and an alarm system. We have enemies."

She shrugged. "Stupid people maybe."

"I don't disagree, honey, but Jack here's one of us. If he needs help, give it to him. And if you see something suspicious, you tell him."

"Suspicious how?"

I said, "Guys who come in who you've never seen before, scoping out the room, paying more attention to how things are done around here than watching you dance."

The big eyes narrowed. "Sorta like…casing the place."

I gave her a smile because she seemed to need one. "That's right. Or if you see somebody who might be dealing."

The big eyes widened. "*Nobody's* dealing shit in *here*."

"Well, if somebody did, it might be to get the club, and Max here, in a jam. A drug bust could shut this place down, and plenty of people would like to see that happen."

Climer was nodding. "Jack's right. We pay good money for beautiful ladies like you to work bottomless, but the cops won't tolerate dealing. The Strip is still workin' its way back from its old junkie-heaven rep."

"Okay," she said indifferently.

He took her hand and whispered, with an urgency that didn't show on the bland baby face: "A drug bust down here means a search warrant for the whole building. That includes upstairs. *Our* upstairs."

Now she got it. She nodded.

Pretty soon she'd gone back to get ready for her set.

I asked him, "What is she on?"

Climer pawed the air. "Nothing hard. Like a lot of these kids, she smokes and does a few lines. She knows I won't tolerate the hard stuff. A good pal of mine O.D.'d on smack. I've seen what it can do. You must've seen that in the service."

"Too much of it."

I wasn't sure about Mavis. No tracks showed on her arms or inner thighs or anything, when she was dancing bare-ass, and with this miner-helmet crowd the bruises and needle marks would show up. Maybe she was just alternating between weed mellow and cocaine high. You go shake your naked pussy or your cock-and-balls at strangers and see if you don't need something.

Climer watched her set, and she showed more energy than the night before; even danced to a ZZ Top tune. A few lines backstage? Then Climer got up from the table and worked the room, moving through the smoke like a ship through fog, shaking hands on his way back to the door in the restroom alcove, to disappear.

Two days later, I'd inhaled a lot of cigarette smoke, nursed beers an hour at a time, and watched a lot of naked girls mime a visit to the gynecologist using pretend stirrups. I did keep an eye on things, such as timing my trips to the john around long-haired patrons making visits there, types who might be doing deals; but when I joined them, nobody seemed to be doing anything but pissing.

On the other hand, I'd noted that Mavis often stopped at the bar to lean across and speak to Leon with some uncharacteristic urgency. Leon gave her apparent queries nothing more than a head shake or nodding response. Nothing suspicious about it, except perhaps the lack of smiles from the professionally friendly Leon.

On the other hand, other dancers stopped to chat with Leon, too, including little Brandi Wyne, AKA Wanda Roux.

The night before I'd had an interesting if brief conversation with Brandi. After her set, in blue bikini and invisible lingerie wrap, she had dropped by my table, all smiles and curves and big pupils.

"So you work here now?" she asked, lifting her eyebrows up and down like we shared a deep dark secret.

"For a week or two, I'll be around."

"Security, huh?"

"Right."

"So the other night…you were upstairs checking out the club's shit for security, huh?"

"I was."

"Didn't really go up there hoping I'd come find you."

"Frankly, no. Glad you did, though."

"So am I. You're different."

A stripper liked me. I was special.

She was saying, "Mostly I'm not into doing things with guys for money."

"Then don't charge them."

She thought about that, then decided to laugh, a little too hard. She touched my hand. "Anyway, welcome to the monkey house. And, uh…if you want to get together some night, maybe we could. You know, not in a money way."

"Sure. I'd like that."

She got up, leaned in to give me a kiss on the cheek, and hustled off toward the hallway that fed the backstage dressing room. What a lovely little body she had.

For now.

Maybe nobody was dealing at the Climax Club, but both Brandi and Mavis were using, and that took its toll. I didn't really get next to any of the other dancers, but wouldn't have been surprised if the whole bottomless bunch of them were doing likewise. Like when you see one roach, you can count on there being a hundred. And you can define roach however you like.

Earlier today, I'd sat with Max Climer in his penthouse office. He was in a light blue CLIMAX polo, smoking a Camel, with a stack of page proofs before him he was in the process of editing. The stereo was playing Marty Robbins, another on the short list of country-and-western artists that didn't send me screaming. The *Gunfighter Ballads* album.

I gave him a report on what I'd observed, which was frankly not much.

"I gather you're not workin' alone," he said.

"No. But you don't need to meet my associate. He won't be on site. Strictly helping me try to locate whoever might be watching you and looking for the right moment."

"'The right moment,' you mean, to put my motherfuckin' lights out."

Even that remark didn't register on his bland, childlike face.

"Yeah," I said. "I'm working on trying to determine who took out the contract, but first order of business is to keep it from getting carried out."

He was frowning; had to look close to tell, but he was. "You know, Quarry, I rarely leave this building, except for occasional meals."

"For now, either learn to cook, or order in…and be careful who's at your door delivering the food."

That made him chuckle; then he noticed I wasn't smiling.

"I'll be downstairs in the club this evening," he said, "at least part of the time."

"Like Bugs Bunny used to say—is this trip really necessary?"

He nodded. "We have a porn star dancin' with us this weekend. Lisa Deleeuw. That always brings out a crowd, but also the protesters, and the TV cameras. I'll have to stick my head outside and give an interview or two."

"Why not invite the media inside?…No. Forget I said that. Your clientele probably wouldn't appreciate the publicity." I sucked some air in and let it out. "Okay. I'll keep one eye on high windows."

"Do that," he said.

Boyd and I had supper at Berretta's BBQ and talked over where we were in this odd-duck assignment.

The restaurant was good-size, one half brightly illuminated and family-oriented, the other with a long curved bar and several booths with low lighting, one of which we took. Soon we were dividing our attention between business and sandwiches piled high with pulled pork, coleslaw and barbecue sauce.

Boyd wiped his mouth with a paper napkin, then wadded it up to join a pile of same. "I've got a good view of the second and third stories of the pawnshop building across from the Climax," he said.

Which was our only real worry. I'd knocked on doors on the two floors of the buildings surrounding the Climax one, using various excuses for bothering what turned out to be the obviously settled tenants of the apartments on the those floors.

"Nobody's in that third-floor apartment," Boyd said. "Not a renter or a squatter."

I asked him, "Are we on top of the rooftops, no pun intended?"

"I got 'em covered from the pad. I have to move from the front window to the side one now and then, but that's no biggie."

"Okay. I'll be on foot, checking cars and such."

He grinned, his mustache dripping with sauce. "Sounds like a plan."

"You got some here," I said, pointing to my upper lip.

"Oh. Thanks, Quarry." He tended to it.

I wasn't getting any of the stuff on my face. As far as you know.

That evening, in the Climax Club, Max Climer was circulating like a good host, stopping at tables to chat. He was wearing a black leather vest over a black-and-red paisley shirt, matching leather pants and pointed-toe cowboy boots. At seven P.M., the joint was already crowded, but otherwise it was the usual smoky scene. The only change was the absence of miner helmets—the visiting screen star did a full strip, but lights shining on her nether regions might display a lack of decorum.

And if some TV crew took advantage of an open-door moment and managed to sneak a shot of such crudity, they would be quick to air it (with some censoring, of course) and ignite even more social outrage from a public eager to see more.

I spent little of my time inside the bar, however, positioning myself instead across the street, windbreaker covering the nine mil in my back waistband, as I leaned against the pawnshop's side exterior wall, taking in the show.

First to arrive was a group who emerged from down the

street on the Climax side of the block, a flock wearing choir robes and a general air of hysteria, waving placards with such pithy sayings as, PORNOGRAPHY IS SOCIAL CANCER, PROTECT OUR CHILDREN — FIGHT PORNOGRAPHY, and PORNOGRAPHY MAKES YOU A SLAVE — GOD SETS YOU FREE.

A little long-winded, I thought ("porn" or "smut" would be better), and the signs weren't handmade—they were print-shop stuff. A spontaneous demonstration this was not.

The timing was perfect—just as the choir reached the front entry of the Climax, waving their signs, and chanting, "Porn is the devil's work," the TV vans rolled in—local NBC, CBS, ABC...Action News, News 5, Eyewitness News. The long-haired crew members, in their untucked polos and jeans, looked more like candidates for Climax Club patrons than representatives of the press; but the on-air reporters were all pretty young women (good call!), who in their professional attire were the opposite of their unclad sisters within. A sound man would stay behind with his equipment at the rear of an open van while cameramen with bulky portable, microphone-strapped cameras on their shoulders followed the female on-air personalities into the breech, as each station's brave pair braved the screaming, sign-waving choir, every would-be Barbara Walters seeking out some representative loon to question.

Finally Climer came out on the doorstep of his sin palace and answered questions in a deadpan serious way, with all three local stations gathering around him in mini-news conference fashion, while the religious ralliers yelled louder, which only helped the devil they despised in making what I assume was his standard Freedom of Speech spiel.

I almost missed the black vinyl-topped Fleetwood Cadillac limo rolling up to the curb on my side of the street. It parked with the motor running. The windows were tinted, but lightly, so I could make out the two thuggish shapes in the front seat, in suit and tie, and another, much more vague shape in back.

Only for an instant did I think this was a surveillance vehicle. Make that a fraction of an instant. No matter how high-priced, a pair of hitmen would neither have the financial wherewithal nor the stupidity to use a Cadillac limousine on stakeout.

But it took me a whole ten seconds to figure out who the guy in back of the limo most likely would be.

I leaned in on the passenger side of the big vehicle and knocked on the window. A face swung my way and frowned at me, the forehead a thick shelf under which small dark eyes lurked; with short slicked-back hair, clean-shaven, he was threatening without trying.

I smiled and made a roll-the-window-down motion with a finger. He thought about the request, frowned a little, and powered down the window, no rolling necessary.

The small dark eyes got smaller, which was his way of saying, *Yes?*

I showed him the nine millimeter and the eyes got larger.

I said, "I work security for the Climax Club, gentlemen. Would you please step out of the vehicle and stand for a search? We've had death threats."

A voice from the rear of the vehicle came, a resonant, liquid baritone with a practiced pleasantness built in. "That won't be necessary, young man. I'm the Reverend Lesser Weaver. Join me in back. We'll talk."

I heard the doors at the rear of the vehicle unlock themselves by way of invitation.

Replacing the nine mil in my back waistband, I threw the tiny-eyed thug a look that probably didn't worry him a whole hell of a lot. Then I opened the sidewalk-side rear door and got in, taking the fold-down seat facing my host, who wore a gray tailored suit, a white shirt, and silk lavender tie with matching breast-pocket hanky.

The leader of the Evangelical Redeemer Church was thin, fifty-something, with money-green eyes, a long Roman nose, a wide mouth, a cleft chin rivaling Kirk Douglas, and a full head of brown hair so styled and sprayed it might have been rubber, like the fake dog shit you can buy in a magic shop.

"You have a name, son?"

"Jack."

"No surname?"

"Quarry."

"Unusual."

"I like it."

"Well, it is distinctive. The Lord likes individuals."

"I thought he preferred sheep."

"We're all sheep before Him."

"Swell. Just keep your shears to yourself. What's your business here, Reverend?"

His eyebrows were darker brown than his hair; he lifted one. "'I say to you that everyone who looks at a woman with lust for her has already committed adultery with her in his heart.' Matthew Five, twenty-seven eight. *That* is my business, young man."

I glanced around the limo interior. "Seems to pay pretty well."

A mild, condescending smile came to the wide, narrow lips. "Our Heavenly Father does not wish poverty upon His servants. He wishes only the best for His followers. 'Delight yourself in the Lord, and He will give you the desires of your heart.' Psalms thirty-seven four."

"Jeez, that sounds a little dirty. But who am I to judge? I was serious about those death threats, Reverend. Do you know anything about that?"

The smile grew even more patronizing, somehow, and the green eyes hardened. "I know that Mr. Climer is at risk of reaping what he's sown."

"If you're talking about sex, I'm pretty sure he does a lot of sowing without reaping. As for making money off the weaknesses of others, I would imagine that's something you know something about."

The smile disappeared. "Perhaps we don't have anything to discuss, young man."

"I think we do. Let's discuss what *you* may reap—you and those two ex-military guys in the front seat, and any other others like them who may be in your employ—if you attempt to kill the man I'm working for."

His laugh was light but somehow chilling. "Kill that pitiful evil pornographer? Why I on earth would I want to do that? I will leave his punishment to the Good Lord's devices."

"Spare me any man-of-God nonsense. It's clear your opposition to Climer's business is getting you a lot of attention from the media. It's a hell of a recruiting tool for your church."

The reverend gestured toward the street, where Climer had gone back in and the choir was chanting, "*God is love, porn is hate.*"

He said, "Yes it is, Mr. Quarry. A most effective recruitment vehicle. Which is exactly why, in addition to the Sixth Commandment, what you're suggesting is absurd. Mr. Climer is helping me build a national congregation. I'm already on the radio, blessed by one hundred thousand watts. I'll be on television…again, nationally…by this time next year."

"You should really draw an audience with that snake-handling routine of yours. And the talking in tongues."

His smile was tinged with regret. "I'm afraid we've had to abandon certain of the more colorful aspects of our preaching to become a more mainstream ministry. Serpents are restricted to the printed page of Genesis now. Speaking the language of angels or ancient forgotten tongues, though, if not overused, that *does* have value."

"Showmanship, you mean."

His shoulders winged up. "Showmanship is but a means to bring troubled souls to the Lord." He folded his hands in his lap as if about to lead me in prayer. "Are you familiar with All-Star Wrestling, young man?"

"Who isn't?"

"What makes that modern-day gladiator spectacle work, would you say?"

I knew what he meant immediately. "A villain. Everybody loves a villain. TV *really* loves a villain."

"Yes. And Max Climer, Mr. Quarry, is mine.…Ah, here come reinforcements."

Charging around the corner, from the same direction as had the choir-robed protesters, a group of young women surged, bearing their own placards, very much not the print-shop variety: PORN KILLS; PORN IS VIOLENCE AGAINST WOMEN; WOMEN AGAINST PORN; porNO!; and even STOP CLIMAXING!, which might or might not have been purposely ambiguous. A banner on poles required two young women to hold it up, both black and in Angela Davis Afros: WOMEN'S LIBERATION NOW! Circled power fists were drawn on either side of the slogan.

The most interesting thing about this second wave of protest was the way the first wave moved back for them, and almost politely, discreetly returned around the corner the way they came. It was a little like watching the offense come off the football field and the defense come on.

"Talk about strange bedfellows," I said.

These new arrivals appeared to be college girls, and they were in jeans and t-shirts or mini-dresses and sandals, lots of long straight hair and round wireframe glasses and no make-up. They were chanting, *"Porn kills!"*

"You coordinated this," I said to Weaver, mildly astonished and definitely impressed. "How did you manage it? These girls are the same pro-abortion bunch your people despise!"

"Where pornography and Max Climer are concerned," he said, with a small shrug, "we share common ground. I have friends on campus who know how to pull strings, and push buttons. These young people came on foot and in their own cars and vans. Our church brought in two busloads. A friendly merchant provided his parking lot."

The TV cameras were still rolling, and the female on-air reporters were finding interview subjects among the rather shrill protesters. No Climax customers entered or left while act two of the show was underway, but then the place had been packed already, with plenty to drink and no shortage of naked women to look at. Everybody was getting what they came here for.

Unlike the choir from Evangelical Redeemer Church, the libber contingent had an apparent leader right there in the thick of the fray, a particularly attractive young woman whose blonde-highlighted brown hair was straight and to her shoulders; she was in cutoffs and a light blue t-shirt that said

FREEDOM OF THE PRESS
IS NOT
FREEDOM TO OPPRESS,

a billboard made all the more appealing by the bra-free nature of her high perky breasts. Two steps led up to a small porch at the

Climax Club entrance, and that's where she stood, addressing the crowd, raising and waving a clenched fist as she led the group of several dozen pissed-off coeds in chanting, *"Porn kills! Porn kills!"*

The door behind her opened and, of all people, Vernon Climer in a denim suit with a winged-collar blue-and-white paisley shirt came out and the girl turned to him and they screamed in detail at each other. Then he took her by the arm and dragged her into the club.

"Shit," I said.

"Language, Mr. Quarry," the reverend said. "Language!"

I got out of the limo on the street side and edged through the throng of now even more pissed-off women, who were yelling various things at that closed door—no organized chanting now, but plenty of overlapping "Bastard!", "Fucker!", "Son of a bitch!" and the ever-popular "Son of a fucking bitch!"

I made my way through this crowd, never having had less fun having college girls throw their bodies at me, and went inside. The guest artist, a redheaded porno actress in a little transparent green nightie, was doing her thing on stage and the males around the runaway were transfixed by this movie star image, the protesting outside drowned out entirely by a sound system blasting Aerosmith's "Walk This Way."

Vernon was dragging the cute lead protestor through the club, obviously heading back to his office. They disappeared past the DJ booth into the hallway and, when I caught up, the door to his office was already closed; but arguing was coming from behind it.

I opened the door and said, "What the fuck is going on? Vernon, you can't just—"

They both looked at me hatefully, though the hatred was left over from their face-to-face confrontation and had nothing at all to do with me, except possibly for some irritation over my interrupting.

Vernon said, "Mr. Quarry, I want you to wait until that crowd of baby harpies flies away, and then drive this young lady home. You do have a car, don't you? She'll tell you the way. Her name is Cordelia. My daughter."

EIGHT

Vernon Climer's little girl Cordelia went along quietly with me, as if I were the police. We found a table near the exit and she sat with her back to the dancer on stage, who happened to be her future aunt, Mavis Crosby, strutting to the Steve Miller Band's "The Joker."

The girl's arms were folded over her perky breasts, making them squish up nicely, her legs crossed and showing plenty of pink flesh in the cutoffs. Her make-up-free prettiness, including big brown eyes, a button nose and a pouty mouth, made her a lot more attractive than Mavis or really any other stripper that her Uncle Max employed.

Sally, the good-looking redheaded waitress I'd got to know some (strictly platonic), came over, unbidden, and dropped the girl off a glass of Sprite and me a Coors. Sally threw me an amused look that said, *What have you got yourself into now, Cowboy?*

I gave her back a look that said, *Who the fuck knows?*

Here I sat, across from Cousin Vernon's daughter, looking at her and not the beanpole with store-bought boobs working the runway. I was trying, frankly, to unsettle this child a little.

And, yes, I was fully aware that this child was only a few years younger than me.

We were well into the next song ("Maggie May") when I said, "If you want to fly out that door and find your own way home, I won't stop you."

She frowned a little, more in confusion than anything else.

I went on: "I don't work for your father. I'm just doing security consulting for Max Climer, working a few weeks to try to whip this dump into shape."

Reluctantly, she met my eyes. "In shape how?"

"Well, right now it's easier to break in this place than getting in one of these strippers' pants. I'm fixing that. The former not the latter."

She thought about whether to be offended or amused, and didn't seem to be able to make her mind up, either way.

"I can use a ride," she said. "What's your name?"

"Jack. Jack Quarry."

She winced, trying to hear me over Rod Stewart. "*What* did you say your last name was?"

"Quarry."

The sullen pout turned into a small but definite smile. "Funny. My name, nickname, is Corrie. That's what I thought you said at first."

"So, then, marriage is out."

The big brown eyes popped. "What?"

"Corrie Quarry. That just doesn't make it."

She'd been sipping her Sprite and her laugh made her snort it out her nose.

I laughed at her, and she didn't mind.

We were briefly between strippers, with only the DJ's voice to compete with anything going on outside. But nothing seemed to be, and the lights of the TV mini-crews were no longer sneaking in and around the edges of the pink window curtains.

"I think it's settled down out there," I said. "You want to go?"

"You're sure the demonstration's over?"

"Why, does it matter?"

"I…I don't want to have to answer certain questions."

"Who from? The media's gone."

"From…from the friends I came with."

"…Having to do with who your father is?"

She swallowed and nodded. "Nobody in the group knows."

"The group?"

"The University of Memphis Liberated Women's Collective."

Catchy.

I asked, "Nobody associates Cordelia Climer with Max and Vernon Climer?"

Her pretty face hardened a little. "I don't use 'Climer.' My mother remarried. It's Cordelia Colman now."

"Nice ring to it. But how does you going up against your father hurt your standing with the other girls?"

Her eyebrows went up. "Girls?"

"Why, was that a mixed group? I didn't remember seeing any guys out there waving signs."

She turned her head sideways and her tone became patronizing. "I haven't been a 'girl' for a very long time."

"Well, it doesn't show."

She glared at me. "Not since I was *thirteen*, I haven't."

"So what are you now?"

"What the fuck do you think? A young woman!"

"Ah. Got you. So. Why wouldn't the other young women respect you all the more for taking on your own father?"

She shrugged. Her eyes were looking past me. That was all the answer I was going to get, at the moment anyway.

Then she said, "Maybe you could just drive me home now."

I said sure and got to my feet. I thought about taking her arm as she rose, but thought better of it. She led the way, her shapely little bottom in the cutoffs pulling male eyes away from the current stripper on stage, the cheeks instinctively rising and falling piston-like to "Brown Sugar."

Then we were out in an evening that had turned to night, and a night that had turned damn near chilly. The scene now was drastically different: no news vans, no protestors, not even a black Caddy limo parked at a curb.

She followed me across Highland to the side street where the pale-green '69 Mustang convertible was parked, its top up.

Her smile suddenly took on a nicely childlike tinge.

"I like it," she said, appraising the ride with her hands on her hips and all politics gone from her brain. The big brown eyes traveled from the Mustang to my face and back again. "Is it too cold, do you think, to put the top down?"

I said it wasn't and did.

Gentleman that I was, I opened her door for her. Hypocrite that she was, she let me.

Behind the wheel, not starting the engine yet, I asked, "Would you like to get something to eat?"

She smirked. "What is this, a date?"

"No. It's that I haven't eaten and if you haven't either, we could do that together, and I could probably get reimbursed by your father for it. What do you say? Shall we stick it to the man?"

We wound up ten minutes away in a beer-and-burger joint called Huey's. The walls were cluttered with nostalgic junk and the tables had red-and-white checkered tablecloths as if it were an Italian joint. The clientele seemed to be mostly white, so I figured the Huey on the sign wasn't Newton. Whoever was responsible, the burgers were thick and a perfect medium rare. We were at a side table in a corner with good privacy.

"To be honest," she said, "I'm a little embarrassed about my father."

"Because he's making a living exploiting women, you mean."

The jukebox was about a decade behind, but I didn't mind.

That was high school and those were good years. Swim team and sock hops. "Just Like Me" was playing.

Squirmingly, she said, "Well, of course, how he makes his money embarrasses me, but…" She sighed, dipping a french fry in catsup. "…he pays my tuition. He pays the rent on my apartment."

"You're not in a dorm?"

"No, I'm a senior, and anyway I don't like roommates. You get assigned somebody and you're just stuck with them. No, Daddy fixed me up with a new pad near the campus. In many respects he's been very good to me."

"But you feel like you're letting him pay your freight with, what? Dirty money?"

She leaned forward, her expression so earnest it hurt to look at. "Jack, I'm not anti-sex or anything. Where do you think the whole Free Love movement started, but on campus?"

I kind of thought Hugh Hefner started it, and guys like this girl's uncle just kicked it into inevitable high gear. You can't get the genie back in the bottle, particularly if it's Barbara Eden.

But I figured I should keep that to myself.

She was saying, "Our group is accepting of all forms of love, including gay and interracial, *any* sexual contact that's adult and consensual. Free Love is about keeping the government out of the bedroom, keeping their grubby hands off sex before marriage, sex *in* marriage, birth control, abortion, even adultery."

Right then I was wondering how her group encouraging the government to ban pornography fit into this line of thinking.

She answered without my having to ask: "But what my father and uncle are involved with exploits sexuality in general and *women* in particular. Do I have to tell you that the Climax Club is a viper's den of drug addiction and prostitution?"

That word viper suddenly brought to mind those snake-handling religious zealots who shared her feminist group's aversion to pornography.

I just listened to her go over the party line and enjoyed my burger. It was juicy and the cheese riding it had a nice sharpness, the grilled onions sweet and crunchy. Once again, my fountain Coke was perfect. This was one great town to eat in. She was letting her burger get cold, doing all that talking.

"Jack, we've done the research—the vast majority of those girls on stage…"

"Young women," I corrected.

"…young women on stage," she said, taking no offense, as if I were being helpful and not a smartass, "have long histories in their short lives of abuse, often of incest. They've been raped, going back to their early teens…even before! And it's left them terribly damaged. They've learned to believe that they have nothing to offer but their sexuality. They're seeking the approval and the shabby love of these grotesque substitute fathers, who toss them lecherous looks and crumpled dollar bills!"

I was working lazily at my fries. "Don't these screwed-up girls…young women…have a right to make a living, the best they can?"

Her eyes showed white all around. "Not when they're being *exploited*!"

"But shouldn't it be up to them? You want some dessert?"

"No. No, I don't want dessert." She was shaking her head. "I'm surprised to hear you talk like that."

"What's wrong with dessert?"

"Nothing! I mean, justifying these girls…women…stripping in public, doing obscene gymnastics for the benefit of a bunch of, of drooling cretinous…" She fought to find the word, then came up with the perfect one. "…*men*!"

"We could share the coconut cream."

"Oh…oh, all right!"

We ordered one piece, two forks.

"Corrie," I said, "those men are sad souls, too. They're just looking for some companionship, and they're paying top dollar for not much of it."

"Don't be silly."

I kept my voice friendly, not teasing. "Come on. Don't you have any compassion for some guy who can't see a pretty girl naked without paying for it? Or who lives a loveless marriage, tied to a woman who doesn't want sex anymore but still expects her man to haul home a paycheck?"

"That's sexist drivel. You're making the *women* out as the exploiters in the Climax Club equation."

"In a way they are."

Her frown had disappointment in it. "I would never have taken you for a misogynist."

"What's that?"

"A woman hater."

I waved that off. "That's not what I am. What's the word for thinking all people are shits?"

"…Misanthrope."

"That's a good one. I'll have to remember that."

She narrowed her eyes at me. "You've never heard that word before? How is that possible? You seem articulate enough. You *do* read books, don't you? From time to time?"

"Sure I do. But words like that don't turn up all that often in Louis L'Amour and Ian Fleming."

Or, for that matter, in *Climax Magazine*.

The pie came. We shared it, as planned. The intimacy was a little awkward but overall nice. The pie itself made life worth living.

She was studying me, trying not to look like it, just sneaking peeks. Finally she asked, "You think *all* people are terrible?"

"No. There's decent ones. And the terrible ones usually have some decency left in them. It's definitely a mixed bag."

Leaning forward earnestly again, she said, "So then you see what happens in a place like the Climax Club as, what? *Understandable*, because *all* people are terrible?"

I met her gaze. "No. I see what goes on there as consensual. And isn't that what the Free Love Movement is all about?"

She sighed, shook her head. "Those dancers make dates with customers and get paid for sex, Jack. That's prostitution! It spreads disease and misery and…and…"

"And it's consensual. The worst thing you can say about what your uncle Max does for a living is that he's crass."

"He's *crass*, all right! He's vulgar and crass and…and…"

Other diners were starting to look at us a little. The jukebox was playing, "I'm a Believer."

"Vulgar and crass covers it," I said. "You and your father are obviously at loggerheads. But what about you and your uncle?"

She seemed to subtly shift gears. "Oh, I've always got along fine with Max. He was nice when I was a little girl. Always had candy for me."

I grinned. "He wasn't offering it from the back of a van, by any chance?"

She choked on some iced tea. "No, he wasn't that kind of uncle. He was always funny and nice. Generous with presents and things, and would sit and talk to you like a person. That's the only thing that makes me kind of feel bad about, you know, demonstrating outside his club."

"You've done that before?"

"Many times."

"You're just giving him free advertising on the news, you know."

"We don't look at it that way!" She sighed. "But I do feel bad. Still, he always *was* a redneck, a hick, whereas Daddy went to college and everything."

I leaned in, really keeping my voice down. "Listen, this security job I'm doing…it involves some serious threats against your uncle."

Alarm widened the brown eyes. "Really?"

"Yes. Is there anybody in your women's group who is a little… too extreme? Who might actually try to hurt Max? Even…really do him harm? Does that sound crazy?"

She took the question seriously. No laughing it off.

"I guess you know," she said, "a few years ago…on campuses like ours…some radical groups really got out of hand…blew up ROTC buildings and so on. But, Jack, I promise you…we aren't militant. We're dedicated. But not violent."

I picked up the check—no argument from my feminist companion—and back in the Mustang, we headed toward her apartment building, the Claridge at Florence and Madison. She smiled into the breeze that made a trailing mane of her blonde-touched brunette hair. A lovely girl. Young woman.

I found a place on the street just down from the venerable but well-maintained '20s-era red-brick seventeen-floor apartment building. Across the street sprawled the University of Memphis campus—this was expensive housing, about as handy as you could get.

Daddy treated his little girl/woman well.

She swung toward me. "You want to walk me up?"

"Sure."

On the sidewalk, we walked side by side, close enough that we brushed a shoulder against each other occasionally. Political talk aside, I could tell she liked me. And I could tell I liked her. She had a lot of ideas, which meant something was going on between her ears, and she hadn't been ruined by life yet. That was refreshing.

The marble-floor lobby was all trendy art galleries and funky shops, for and by hippies with dough. A pharmacy called Maggie's was still open and it was almost ten, for those interested in legal drugs. We took an elevator that was spacious enough for a uniformed operator to have once ridden with us comfortably.

At the door of her seventh-floor apartment, we stood awkwardly, like junior high kids on a first date.

"You want to come in for a minute?"

"Sure," I said. "For a minute."

It was an efficiency apartment—one large room with kitchenette, living-room area with sleeping quarters tucked off to one side, with a separate bathroom of course. The furnishings were Danish modern and the walls were decorated with posters —Einstein sticking his tongue out, Mr. Spock from *Star Trek*, "We Can Do It!" (Rosie the Riveter making a muscle), a PEACE poster with matching symbol. Off-campus or not, this was a dorm room. A rich girl's dorm room—not a grown woman's apartment.

The lighting was low, just a table lamp, on an end table on which I discreetly deposited my nine millimeter wrapped in the windbreaker. We plopped onto a couch that was more comfortable than it looked and she asked me if I wanted to smoke. I didn't figure she meant tobacco. Either way, I said no thanks. She had a pitcher of lemonade in the refrigerator and got us a couple of glasses. A window was letting in nice cool air and some night sounds, muffled traffic but also that breeze ruffling trees.

"You're interesting," she said. "Did you go to college?"

"No. I went to Vietnam."

She thought about that a while, her eyes tight and troubled and excited. "Did you…kill anyone?"

"Yes."

"Does it…bother you?"

"No."

"Why doesn't it?"

"They were there to kill me."

"But…weren't you somewhere where you weren't wanted?"

"Some of them wanted us there. Others didn't. I don't talk about this."

"See…you *are* bothered."

"I bet you protested it."

"What?"

"The war."

"No. It was…kind of before my time."

Shit.

"I'm not a prude," she said. Kind of a non sequitur, but she said it.

"I never said you were. Never thought it, either."

She kissed me. Hard and sudden. I kissed her back and it got softer, sweeter. We necked a while. I slipped my hands under her protest t-shirt, but she didn't protest. Her breasts were warm and soft and round, the tips soft, then hard. She rubbed the front of my jeans.

"See," she said, "I *like* sex."

"I believe you," I said.

We necked and petted for maybe half an hour. After a while I put my hand between her thighs, rubbing the cutoffs over the zipper area. Then she got onto her back and we dry-humped. I started to undo her cutoffs but she grabbed my hand and stopped me, shaking her head. Then we dry-humped some more. Very high school. Kind of charming. But that was as far as it got, and I stopped short of making a mess in my trousers.

She seemed embarrassed when she walked me to the door,

hand in hand. Was it because we'd gone as far as we had, or because that's all the farther she'd allowed us to go?

"I wouldn't mind seeing you again," she said.

"That was the impression I got. What's your number?"

"You want me to write it down?"

"No. I want to remember it."

The erection rode all the way back to the Highland Strip with me. Erection aside, I was oddly excited and a little irritated. I'd been blown by a stripper and humped by a housewife, and now a college girl wasn't letting me go all the way.

How much sex did these people think I could stand?

My parking spot on the side street was waiting for me. The lights were off in the stakeout pad, but I knew Boyd was up there, probably with his binoculars in hand. I pulled in to the space, my hard-on finally getting it into its head that nothing was going to happen right now, and glanced toward the pawn-shop building across the way.

Lights were on behind the shades in the third-floor windows of the unoccupied apartment.

NINE

The sight of Boyd in his nylon pajamas—salmon with black piping—might have amused me had I been in the mood.

But I wasn't, the two of us sitting on the frayed flat-cushioned couch in the living room of the stakeout pad with only the light from the hallway giving us any illumination at all.

Meanwhile, the lights seemed to be on in every window of the third-floor apartment above the pawnshop across from the Climax Club.

Boyd asked, "What do you make of it?"

I was not in my pajamas. I was still in the t-shirt and jeans and windbreaker with the nine millimeter Browning in my rear waistband. Ready to go back out into the fray if need be. If a fray was what was out there.

"Could be a new tenant," I said. "A real one. I can scope that out tomorrow."

"And if it isn't?"

"Then one half of the team has arrived."

"The passive half. The stakeout guy."

"*If* it's a team."

"What do you mean, Quarry?"

"I mean, we're judging everything by the procedures the Broker's people go by. We can't be sure those procedures apply here. It could be a single shooter, doing his own surveillance."

Boyd shrugged. "Or it really could be a stakeout guy, and if so, that means he'll spend anywhere between two days and two weeks, building a pattern for the target."

I thought about it. "If it's a team of two, with a similar M.O.

to ours, the passive half is moving in and getting the pad set up as temporary quarters. Like you say, for maybe as long as two weeks."

"Right."

"Which means the active half, the shooter, will show up some time between a few days and a couple of weeks to get briefed by his backup and maybe do some surveillance himself, before going forward."

Boyd's eyes narrowed. "So probably Max Climer isn't in immediate danger."

"Probably not."

His features clenched and he jerked a thumb toward that third-floor flat. "What if we went over there and just snuffed the son of a bitch? If he's a solo player, so much the better. If he's half of a team, the shooter either hears his backup guy has been killed, and never shows, or even stumbles onto the body himself. In which case, he books it out of Dodge."

I frowned. "And possibly taking a run at Climer before he does."

"No, Quarry, once the gig's gone south, he's gone."

Boyd was probably right.

Still, I said, "We're not hitting the one across the street. Not yet. Not now."

"Okay, then tell Climer he may be in the crosshairs and to be extra damn cautious. You stick with him yourself, as much as possible. He's brought in more ex-biker-boy bodyguards already, right?"

"Yes."

Boyd shrugged. "Cool. Then we operate assuming that the activity across the way is the stakeout guy moving in, and we wait for the shooter to show. When he does, we take them both out. And earn our pay."

I mulled it. Then: "That would give me a little more time to try to pinpoint whoever hired it."

"Exactly. In which case we earn *more* pay. If we go across the street now, and make a mess, this thing is over, for us. Nothing left but a quick exit."

"So instead…"

"…we sit tight. And watch. And wait."

I thought about it some more.

Then I nodded slowly and said, "Sit and watch and wait."

"Right. And Quarry?"

"Yeah?"

"It's your turn."

And Boyd, legs of his nylon jammies rubbing together like a cicada mating call, trundled back off to bed.

So for several hours I watched that third-floor apartment from the stakeout pad. Lights on in there had made the drawn shades glow somewhat and the edges around them were bright. Starting around eleven P.M., however, they gradually went off.

Then the whole place was dark.

It did feel like somebody had moved in, gotten a little settled, and was in for the night.

I watched for another half-hour, using the binoculars, then went down to see if any parked-car surveillance might be happening; but none seemed to be. Edgy, not knowing exactly what I should be doing, I went in the club to see if everything was under control there.

It was. A quarter till midnight found the place starting to thin. Brandi was on stage, bopping to Grand Funk Railroad's "The Loco-Motion," her blue bikini tossed aside like dirty clothes on a teenage girl's bedroom floor. The seats lining the runway were all taken, though only maybe a third of the choreography lovers had sprung for miner's helmets.

Over the past few days, security at the Climax Club building had been beefed up nicely. A locksmith had taken the various doors to college (Yale), a security firm had installed an alarm system with separate keypads on every floor, and half a dozen ex-bikers with permits-to-carry were now on staff. At the moment, some of the latter were acting as additional bouncers in bow ties and tuxedo shirts.

On the upper floors, other former Hells Angels types were at posts positioned to handle any invaders. Wearing big-and-tall men's shop suits that could handle big chests and sizable bellies, the latter group tended to have ponytails and a general Sumo wrestler look, with revolvers clipped to their belts and slightly exploded features with a built-in glower.

I found a table easily and Sally, the friendly redhead waitress in her usual green bikini, came over and delivered a Coors, as usual without asking. I really liked her. Under normal circumstances I would have tried to get to know her better.

She sat next to me. She had the kind of lush mouth with an upper lip that curled back when she smiled. "Surprised to see you, honey," she said.

"Why's that?"

Her shrug lifted her full freckled breasts and set them down with a jiggle. Being a gentleman, I pretended not to notice. "Just figured you'd be with Maxie tonight," she said.

"Why? Where is he?"

"On a little overnight with Mavis." She frowned. "You didn't know? Aren't you his top security guy?"

I put a hand on her bare arm, did my best not to squeeze. "Is Vernon still here?"

"Yeah, of course. In his office in back."

I started to get up and this time she gripped my arm, not worrying about whether it hurt or not. "No, honey, better not—he's in conference. You let me get him for you."

She went off to do that. Instead of enjoying the view, I was trying, unsuccessfully, to wrap my head around Climer running off somewhere without telling me. I told myself to cool it— what appeared to be the passive half of a two-man kill squad had only just tonight installed himself in that third-floor apartment across the way. That meant the hit was not imminent.

Right?

Brandi was off the stage and back out circulating on the club floor in her blue bikini and lingerie wrap, trolling for table dances. She spotted me, her features freezing for a moment as if trying to place me, then did her little-girl grin and waved with wiggling red-nailed fingers. I waved back with my flesh-colored ones and no wiggling.

Something was wiggling in my brain, though, threatening to become a thought.

I watched her walk over to where the same beady-eyed bouncer as on my first visit to the Climax Bar again stood watch, back against the wall by the restroom alcove, looking like a bored harem eunuch. She was whispering to him while he tried to think. Then he whispered to her while she tried to think.

The angle was wrong, damnit—I had picked up lip-reading over the years, taking my turns at surveillance, and while not an expert at the art, I could often make out enough to be helpful. But whispering in each other's ears made these two really bad subjects.

Sally came over and said, "Vernon's just wrapping up his meeting. He'll be out soon."

"What's her name?"

She gave me the curled-upper-lip lip-glossed smile again. Her eyes were as green as her bikini. "You don't know want to know."

"Sally, how long has Brandi worked here?"

The waitress frowned a little. "Well, she doesn't, honey."

"What do you mean, she doesn't?"

Her head bobbed back and forth, her big red hair going along for the ride. "Well, does and doesn't. She's on the circuit. She's featured. We get her about four times a year, month at a shot. This is her last weekend, this time around."

"Oh. Nobody told me."

"Must be you never asked, honey."

Sally got up, gave me a green-eye-shadowed wink, and hip-swung toward the bar, absurd and sublime in bikini with high-heel sandals.

If I'd gone all the way with Vernon's daughter Corrie, earlier tonight, maybe I wouldn't be thinking about how much I'd like to fuck Sally right now. Jesus Christ, I had to get out of this place. This was the kind of job where if a bullet didn't get you, syphilis would.

Speaking of which, Brandi plopped her little bottom down in the chair next to mine and gave me her own lascivious lip-glossed smile. Her big brown eyes were glittering, but with what, I couldn't be sure. *why does every woman in this book have big brown eyes*

"What are you up to later?" she asked, and her eyes widened and half-closed, then widened again. Normal pupils tonight.

"Nothing planned," I said.

"I got a couple table dances to do. Check in with me before you go—I'll be done by one. I'm only here a few more days, you know."

I knew that now.

"Might be our last chance to have a little fun, sugar," she said, pushing up from the table, eyebrows doing the Groucho bit. "And it won't cost you a diddly damn thing."

Then she sashayed off to a waiting customer, leaving me to wonder if there might not be a hidden fee.

A traveling stripper, "on the circuit," would have a perfect built-in cover, should she be in the same business as Boyd and me. She could have taken this gig and was acting as an on-site surveillance person, and those third-floor lights across the street might mean it was the *shooter* who'd shown up.

Or she might be the shooter herself—it'd been chauvinistic of me, downright sexist to assume the one handling the gun had to be a man. Again, she was perfectly positioned to...

Was I fucking nuts?

Did I really believe that little airhead was capable of making it in the murder business? Then I thought about how she'd followed me up to the magazine offices, that first night, and how she checked me out in her own special way. Maybe that bouncer, who I had just seen her whispering to, was her partner in crime. Maybe *he* was a new employee, too.

Then Vernon Climer was making his way through the remains of the Climax Club crowd; he looked mildly disheveled, particularly for a guy who usually seemed to have every hair in place. That hair right now had the look of having been mussed, then quickly combed, his denim suit a little rumpled, blue-and-white paisley shirt wrinkled. Yup. He'd been in conference all right.

Vernon said, "You're wondering where Max and Mavis got themselves off to."

I didn't hide my irritation. "More like, where did they go to get themselves off."

His palms pressed the air, signaling that I should settle down. "Max has a rustic little cabin near Shelby State Park. He has had since before he got rich and famous—a quiet little getaway for times when things get a little too heavy for him."

"And he didn't think to mention this to me?"

Vernon shrugged. "It was a spur-of-the-moment thing. It always is for Max. He grew up in moonshine country, you know, and sometimes he just needs to get next to nature."

"Oh, for Christ's sake…"

"Mr. Quarry, you weren't around to be informed. And, well, we have no way to reach you, do we? Which I have to say strikes me as strange—generally a consultant is somebody you should be able to…consult."

Couldn't defend myself by saying stakeout pads didn't come with phones.

I said, "I want you to take me to this hillbilly haven. Right fucking now."

His eyes tightened. "Mr. Quarry, first of all, I have other business to conduct."

What's her name?

"And second of all, Max is in perfectly good hands. He took two of those new security guards with him, as well as his armed chauffeur."

"How did they travel?"

"In Max's pink Cadillac."

"So, keeping a low profile then."

His expression and voice softened. "Mr. Quarry, thanks to your own commendable efforts, my cousin is perfectly safe. Those bodyguards are armed, and bigger than grizzlies. He will be back by late morning."

"I assume the Cadillac picked him up in the alley behind the building."

"Yes. Down the stairs and right into the vehicle."

Apparently Vernon didn't know how quick and precise a bullet from a high place could be.

I said, "I want detailed directions to that cabin."

"You mean…now?"

"Right now. I'm not local, remember. Keep them simple and clear."

Vernon drew in a deep breath and let it out as a sigh. "I will humor you, Mr. Quarry. For one reason only—because you have done a remarkable job of convincing my cousin of the need for some twentieth-century security measures."

"Not a good enough job, apparently."

He raised his hands in surrender. "I'll write out those instructions."

He went off to do that.

Over near the restrooms, Brandi was again conferring with Bruno, her bouncer friend. But this time they weren't leaning in so close, and both were sneaking looks my way. I was pretending to watch a frosted-haired dancer named Kimberly as she shed her burgundy bikini.

I didn't get much of what they were saying, but what I did get was choice, as Brandi told Bruno: *"Don't worry—I can keep him busy all night."*

That told me everything I needed to know, and what I needed to do.

After Vernon delivered a folded-in-two typed sheet of directions, I ducked out and went across to our stakeout above the dead café, going in the cross-street side way as usual. In Boyd's bedroom, I flipped the light switch. He awoke instantly and his .38 long-nosed revolver, snatched from below the unused pillow to one side, pointed my way, but just briefly.

"Quarry," he said, lowering the gun. "What the fuck?"

I told him what the fuck. That Max Climer and his lady friend Mavis had slipped off for a night away at a cozy cabin in the boonies, and that the hit—or some other screwed-up thing—was going down tonight, while Climer and his main squeeze were isolated in the sticks. Two bodyguards and their driver were with them, either a first line of defense or conspirators. If the latter proved the case, the man we were here to protect might already be dead.

"But I don't think so," I said. "I think a bouncer named

Bruno will be one of the attackers, and possibly somebody else from the club. That little stripper Brandi is in on it and plans to keep me away and busy. She and Bruno may even be the hit team we've been waiting for. As for how that might relate to the activity above the pawnshop, I haven't the slightest damn clue."

He was already out of bed and getting into a thin black long-sleeve t-shirt and black slacks. "Shit," he said. "We should be leaving *now*."

"No. Unless those biker bodyguards and Max's longtime driver really are conspirators, whatever's been planned won't go down for several hours."

"How do you figure?"

"The club closes at two. Bruno will be on for at least another hour after that, helping clean up. It's only ten till one now. I'm going to deal with little Brandi and see what I can get out of her. She's off at one. When I'm finished with her, I'll pick you up out front before two. Be out there waiting at a quarter till."

Boyd's eyes were slits under the shaggy brows. "We don't have a hell of a lot of firepower. I mean, for not knowing what we'll be up against."

"I have a spare nine mil, and the .25."

"I have a spare S & W .38, the short-barrel one."

"They'll have to do. You bring any handcuffs?"

Shortly after one, Brandi headed from the behind-the-stage dressing room toward me where I waited at the bar. She was in a dark-blue-and-pink-and-white floral mini-dress with navy suede Oxfords and gray stockings that went up over her knees, giving her a college-girl look. Actually, the look of a girl who'd never been to college fulfilling her non-collegiate boyfriend's fantasy.

She found my hand and the pink-glossed kiss of a mouth

smiled up at me, aided and abetted by the big brown eyes, pupils large again.

"Let's go to my place," she said. "You have a car, lover? It's a few blocks."

As directed, I drove to the Highland Motel, a two-story number that had seen better days, its neon letters burned down to HIGH____ MOTEL, which even with the Strip reforming its druggie ways was probably accurate.

She led me up cement stairs to the second-floor walkway and used her key to let us in to 209. The room smelled like her, or anyway her musky, floral perfume. The decor was Early Nothing, the walls pale pink. The smallish double bed was made and the open suitcase on a stand was the only sign of occupancy, though a glance into the bathroom showed a counter lined with beauty products and other toiletries. This was indeed her room, not somewhere I was being led into ambush.

"It's nothing to write home about," she admitted, tossing her little clutch purse on a chair. "But it's better digs than most clubs provide the visiting talent. You want anything?"

When I didn't answer immediately, she said, "There's weed and we could do a few lines. Bourbon in my suitcase—Coke machine downstairs."

"No, I'm fine."

She came over and had me unzip her mini-dress in back. "I have to shower, honey. You'll thank me later. Long night!"

"Sure."

She took her blonde hair off—I hadn't spotted it as a wig, an expensive job apparently—and exposed a much shorter blonde cut. The fake hair she tossed on a dresser. Then she shut herself in the bathroom and soon the shower was going.

I took the opportunity to go through her things. No gun in

her purse. Nothing in the suitcase indicated she was in my field of endeavor, either—no weapons, no binoculars, no electronic bugs. Some 8x10's of her in a glittery two-piece stripper outfit, for her to sign, I supposed. Some letters from a sister. A little datebook showing her schedule for the next six months. Bookings of a week, two weeks, a few for a month.

Nothing suspicious.

She emerged naked, toweling off her hair. Somehow it was more erotic than when she'd danced on stage that way. I knew this girl, this young woman, was tasked with keeping me busy so that something bad could happen to a man I was hired to protect. That did not stop me from getting diamond hard in about ten seconds.

Her blonde pubic patch, trimmed back some, was natural, something you don't see every day, with or without a coal miner's helmet. Her high handfuls were perfect, tips hard. Waist, something you could put two hands around. She was toweling off her short blonde hair, and she wore no make-up at all now.

She smiled at me. "What's your pleasure, honey?"

My tongue was as thick as my dick. I said, "I, uh…"

"You want me to put some make-up on? Red lipstick, maybe, like in the old movies? But with the kind of action you won't see on *The Late Show*? No?"

She bent over the foot of the bed, resting herself on a green nubby spread, and offered her backside up for whatever I might have in mind.

"Anywhere you wanna put it's fine, baby. I don't mind. And I'm all clean for you."

"No," I said. "Thanks, but…"

She flipped around and sat on the edge of the bed with her legs spread and her tuft glistening. "Then what *is* your pleasure?"

I was still fully clothed, including my black windbreaker. I slipped a hand in my pocket and brought out the pair of handcuffs. They glistened, too.

Her eyes got so big, the pupils seemed small. Her smile was a devilish thing, even without red movie-star lipstick.

"Kinky," she said. "I wouldn't have taken you for the bondage type."

"I won't hurt you," I promised.

She shook her head; droplets flew off the short hair. "Don't spoil it. Play the game. Keep it real. Punish me. Spank me first, if you want."

"No," I said. "I just want you helpless."

She was into it, her anticipation genuine. This was not perfunctory sex for a john or an employer or even a boyfriend whose needs needed tending before she could get a decent night's sleep. No, I had blundered into one of her favorite bedroom pastimes.

I handcuffed her right hand to a headboard post. Then I revealed the second pair of cuffs and she grinned at me with feral delight. I cuffed her left ankle to the metal frame of the bed.

"Find something else to tie me up the rest of the way," she said, breathing hard.

"Okay," I said.

I took one of pillowcases off and tore it into strips, and tied her other hand to a headboard bedpost and her other ankle to the frame. Her legs were spread very wide indeed.

"Let me see that thing," she said, eyeing the bulge near my zipper.

"Okay," I said, and got the nine millimeter out of my back waistband.

Her lewd smile dissolved into something unsure of itself, and then was gone entirely.

"You aren't going to…" she started. "Don't you put that in me!"

"Please," I said, offended, as I sat on the edge at the bottom of the bed, between her wide-spread legs. "What kind of creep do you take me for?"

She was thinking about that when I started asking her questions.

TEN

The rain came as a surprise, hard and intense. The convertible's cloth top took it well, maybe better than a hardtop's metal roof, the sound not unlike being under an umbrella or in a tent.

But the downpour slowed us down, neither of us familiar with Memphis nor its surrounding environs. I was driving and Boyd navigating, a small flashlight letting him refer both to Vernon Climer's typewritten instructions and a Memphis area map ("Turn right on Lamar Avenue!"). Traffic, at least, was light in the early A.M. hours, but visibility was shit ("Take a right onto the ramp—240!").

What should have taken half an hour or so grew to more than forty-five minutes, as we went from I-40 to US-51, and then to county roads with names like Fite, Island and Ramsey. We were bordering Meeman-Shelby Forest Park, its swampy bottomland edging the Mississippi River, its bluffs thick with oak, ash and beech. By sunlit day, those trees would be blazing with color, like the ones on my lake back home. But right now they were just dark shapes in the wet night.

I had, of course, filled Boyd in on what I'd learned from Brandi.

I'd barely started my paraphrase of my conversation with the stripper when Boyd frowned and said, "What makes you *believe* that treacherous little bitch?"

"She was too scared to lie."

"Oh, please."

"No, really. She thought I was going to stick my nine millimeter up her twat and light up her insides."

After that, Boyd made no further comment on the subject, just taking in what I had to say. And I *did* believe her.

Are you and Bruno here to kill Max Climer?

What? Are you crazy?

That's beside the point. Tell me the truth and I'll give you a pass.

Do I look like a killer?

You look like somebody the Indians staked out for the killer ants to get.

You're a terrible, awful, fucking fucker!

Again, not an issue. If it's not to kill the man, what then? What is supposed to happen tonight?

Well, it's not *killing* somebody!

What then?

Bruno and his friend Eddie, you know, that bartender?

Go on.

They're just going to, you know, take him.

Take him.

Grab him. Take him off somewhere.

Kidnap him, you mean.

If you wanna put it that way.

For ransom?

Well, for money.

How much?

Five-hundred thou. I mean, we work downstairs for peanuts and Max is just upstairs one fuckin' floor making millions off of pussy photos! Is that fair? Why shouldn't people like us get a little taste?

Five hundred grand is a gulp, not a taste. What exactly is the plan, Brandi?

"They have somebody on the inside," I told Boyd. "One of the new guys, the biker-crowd bodyguards. His name is Larry."

"Are the others Moe and Curly?"

The windshield wipers were working hard. "She didn't know the details, but somehow Larry is supposed to have things ready for Bruno and Eddie. Ready so they can grab Max and go, nice and quick."

"What about that Mavis broad?"

"Don't know. Didn't come up."

"She say what kind of vehicle they were in?"

"Yeah. A panel truck, a Ford, dark green."

"Late as we're running," Boyd said, "keep an eye out for that Ford, coming our direction. We may have to improvise."

"No argument."

A few minutes went by with nothing but the sound of those wipers and more pattering on the softtop.

Then Boyd said, "This could still be the hit, Quarry. Just because your little hooker-stripper seems to be telling the truth, they might be using her, helping to set Climer up for the kill."

"I know it."

Even with the rain trailing off into drizzle, things got trickier for us, because now we were dealing with unmarked backroads and lanes. After a while, I was thinking we'd screwed up till I saw the sign beside a graveled byway that said, TRESPASSERS WILL BE SHOT AND EATEN. This tallied both with Max Climer's dark, rustic sense of humor and with the most bizarre part of his cousin's typewritten directions.

We rolled slowly up the slight gravel incline so as not to crunchily announce our approach. Halfway along what Vernon's notes said was a quarter-mile lane, we pulled over. I had insisted that Boyd take my spare nine mil as his primary weapon, because it had a silencer. He'd traded me his spare .38 S & W, and of course I had the little .25.

Boyd was in ninja black, assuming his red-and-yellow Peter Max jockey shorts didn't ride up in back, and I was in the black windbreaker and jeans. We would blend into the night well enough. The rain had done us a favor, because I wanted to angle through the trees, an approach that would have been an even noisier one than on the gravel, before the rain wetted down the leaves under our feet.

The walk seemed longer than it was, as we moved through trees that still had plenty of leaves to rustle and flick droplets at us. It was damn near cold. Finally we came up onto the promised clearing where the cabin perched above a river view we couldn't see. A few lights were on in the two-story log-wood structure, the front of which faced us across a leaf-strewn gentle slope and a gravel apron that opened up from the lane to provide some parking. The pink Cadillac was off to one side as was a blue-and-white Dodge Charger that probably belonged to the security guys, or one of them anyway, who followed Max, Mavis and their driver out here. Another vehicle was pulled up right along the front porch.

A dark-green Ford panel truck.

We approached quickly, cautiously, staying low, moving across the damp, not noisy leaves, heading toward the near side of the structure, by the gas tank and some windows. Along the way we noted no one through the windshield of the van, and nobody standing outside or on the porch with its tiled overhang, pine posts and rocking chairs. Apparently those who'd arrived in that vehicle were inside.

The cabin was not the rustic affair that I had pictured when Vernon Climer spoke of his cousin's moonshine roots and need to get back to nature. This was a log cabin, all right, but two sizeable stories of one, and—peeking through a window onto a fully outfitted kitchen—I could see a knotty-pine-paneled world that included a cozy living room with chocolate leather sofas and chairs arranged around a stone-facade gas fireplace. Open pine-wood stairs to the second floor demarcated the two big downstairs areas.

At a cedar log table in the kitchen, three big men wearing *Climax Magazine* polo shirts (pink) sat, slumped on their elbowed arms, sleeping or otherwise unconscious. Playing cards were scattered toward the center of the table, filled ashtrays here and there, with a coffee cup near each slumbering man.

One of these men may not have been sleeping. He might be named Larry, and he might have prepared the bodyguards for the evening's scheduled activity by drugging their coffee. He may have done the same thing for Max and Mavis, presumably upstairs in a bedroom, although possibly with hot chocolate or an alcoholic beverage, since people getting ready for sleep might not drink coffee. Whether he had drugged his own coffee (or whatever was in the bodyguards' cups) to better seem a victim himself, or was simply pretending, I'd yet to establish.

I felt Boyd's hand squeeze my arm as he drew my attention through the window away from the men at the table and toward three other men, who were coming down the open pine stairs. Two were big boys in running suits and dark stocking masks with only their eyes showing; they had what looked to be .357 Magnum handguns in their gloved right fists.

One big man was dragging down those stairs a groggy-looking Max Climer, wearing a flung-on black silk robe, his legs and feet bare; the other was following, brandishing his Magnum.

I gave Boyd a head wag and he followed me around front. We could hear them moving inside. They'd be across to the front door and onto the porch in seconds. I indicated the van and Boyd trailed after as I headed back behind. The rear van doors were unlocked. We got in, closing ourselves in, moments before we heard the cabin's front door open and the two big men come out, dragging Max Climer.

Climer was objecting but in a slurry manner, befitting a guy who'd been doped.

"Fuck's going on?" he was saying. "Outa your fuckin' skulls." And so on.

We waited. Footsteps on gravel. Muffled voices spoke to their captive (muffled because of the masks, not distance).

"Behave yourself, everything gonna be cool. This is just a money deal. You don't gotta die."

"Yeah," the other one said, "you just go along and we get along, everything be fine and jim dandy."

One van door swung open, and then so did the other. Apparently both abductors were going to help their captive up and in. I was at right against a van wall and Boyd was backed to the left wall, each of us with a silenced nine millimeter Browning in hand, and the two big men in ski masks froze momentarily upon seeing us—Max, I don't think, saw us at all—and Boyd put a bullet in the head of the one nearest him, and I put a bullet in the head of the one nearest me. The two clouds of blood mist created by our nearly simultaneous shots mingled and dissipated.

The two silenced-gun reports made small raspy coughs, reverberating a little in the van but not making it outside, where the two men were tottering on feet that had stopped receiving signals from their brains, organs that had never been that impressive in the first place. The last decision those minds made was a reflexive one, which was to dump their owners on their dead asses, leaving Max Climer standing there, with wide glassy eyes, tottering a little himself.

"Inside," I told Boyd. "One of those three at the table could be faking."

Boyd quickly jumped down out of the van, landing at the feet of the man he'd killed, and hustled inside. A second later I followed, taking Climer by the arm and guiding him along.

"Max, you've been drugged," I said. "Take it easy and you'll come out of it."

"You…you killed those pricks."

"Yeah, that was a kidnap try. They didn't make it."

Inside, Boyd was standing a few feet away from the log table where the three security guys were slumped like kids in school at nap time.

"Larry!" I said.

One of the three made an involuntary twitch. I hadn't known which one was Larry, but I did now. I went over and dragged him out of the log chair. Like all of these guys, he was big, big shoulders, big arms, big belly. But I had adrenalin on my side, and a silenced nine mil in his neck, so we were more than evenly matched. I walked him, shoved him, back into the pine counter that housed a sink and dishwasher and other things that probably weren't in the cabin of Max Climer's childhood.

Larry had a flat nose and freckles and rusty, clumpy hair above a wide brow, with cow eyes fringed with strangely pretty long lashes. His teeth were oversize, tobacco-stained, and his lips were thick. Larry was an ugly motherfucker.

"Bruno and Eddie are dead," I said.

The cow eyes bulged further.

"I mean, that *was* Bruno and Eddie in those masks, right?"

"Don't know what you're talkin' about." His voice was breathy and high-pitched and, like the pretty lashes, undermined his tough-guy image.

"They're dead," I repeated. "And that makes them a problem. For us, and for you."

"I…I don't understand."

"The snatch went south, got it? If the cops get you, they'll have you on felony murder, because Bruno and Eddie died committing a felony that you were part of."

"I didn't commit a fucking felony! Since when is drugging drinks a felony?"

I ignored the question. "Your employer, Mr. Climer, can't be having dead bodies littering up his place. It's unsanitary and it raises questions, should anybody notice. So we have to get rid of the bodies."

He was trying to back away, but the gun in his throat just followed. "Go ahead! I'm not stopping you!"

"Larry, you're the only one who's still alive, so you're elected to help out. You're going to drive that van where I tell you, and then we'll dump it and its passengers. My friend here will follow us, and we'll ride back and you can go on with your life."

"You'll just kill me, too!"

I shrugged. "Maybe not. It's just that there's a mess that needs cleaning up, and you can help. You'll rack up some serious brownie points, doing that."

There was a little more talk, but I supervised while Boyd and Larry loaded the two dead men—who, with their stocking masks pulled off, indeed turned out to be Bruno and Eddie—into the back of the van. My nine mil nudged Larry in the back as I walked him to the driver's side. He got in. Boyd covered him while I came around and got in on the rider's side.

I had told Climer to make himself some coffee and wait for us. If his boys came out of their slumber, he should explain that Bruno, Eddie and Larry had attempted an ill-advised kidnap, and his security chief, me, was taking care of the aftermath. But telling them nothing more. I also let him know that we'd be gone for a while, because we needed to dump the bodies well away from his cabin. He seemed neither shocked nor surprised.

Boyd hustled down the gravel lane to where we'd left my Mustang. I gave him a chance to do that, then told Larry to start the engine. Soon we were moving along on a deserted county road and Boyd had fallen in behind us.

"Where are we going?" Larry asked.

"Just drive. I'll tell you."

Truth was, I didn't know. I was just keeping track of where we were, and noting a landmark every time I had him turn, plus making sure we always ended up heading north, memorizing the names of the various roads (Lock, Walsh, Campbell) on the impromptu route.

Larry stole a look at me. "You…you didn't have to kill those two."

"Sure I did. Kidnapping's a capital offense."

"It is?"

"Ever since Lindbergh."

"Who?"

"Just drive."

He drove.

A few miles later, he said, "You're not the law."

"What's that got to do with shit?"

"If it's a capital offense, you ain't the one pulls the switch."

"That's a good point, Larry. You're new at the Climax Club, aren't you?"

He nodded, the thick-lipped puss more relaxed now. "But I knew Bruno from way back. I played football with him at North Side High, till I dropped out."

"Sorry for your loss."

"Huh?"

"Him dying earlier."

"Oh. Yeah. Well, he was always gettin' in trouble. I shouldn'ta listened to him. Shouldn'ta got involved in this."

"No."

"You think Mr. Climer will fire me?"

"Well, you did try to kidnap him."

"No, I just drugged the coffee and drinks. I didn't know what Bruno and that Eddie was gonna do."

"Maybe not kidnap him."

"Yeah. Maybe not."

"Probably just rob the place."

"Probably. Yeah."

"Or maybe kill Max. And then they'd have had to kill you as a witness."

"Oh, no. I don't think Bruno would go *that* far."

I shrugged. "Well, you never know about people."

"That's for dang sure."

"Over here."

"Just pull 'longside the road?"

"Please."

He did. Boyd pulled in behind him.

He looked over at me. "Now what?"

I shot him between the cow eyes and pretty lashes. Apparently something had been in his head, because it splashed against the side window. He fell against the wheel, thankfully not honking the horn, and stared at me with a hurt expression.

Couldn't blame him.

I let Boyd stay at the wheel of the Mustang on the way back. I'd paid fairly close attention to the haphazard path I'd taken, but he felt confident about having it down, so I deferred.

We'd been gone an hour.

The two security guys, whose names were Cliff and Rick, were sitting at the table with new, undrugged coffee cups, but still looking groggy. In his black silk robe, Climer was seated with them, with his own coffee cup, looking close to alert by now. Boyd pulled up a chair. I didn't. I wanted to loom a little.

"Gentlemen," I said, "three men were killed tonight in an

attempt to kidnap your boss. Right now they are waiting to be found by the roadside in the van they arrived in. Does anyone have a problem with that?"

No one said anything, but the two security guys didn't seem quite so groggy suddenly.

"I took the initiative," I continued, "assuming you would agree that Mr. Climer did not need these three dead men in his life. He has enough problems right now with lawsuits and demonstrators and so on that adding the police to that list would be less than helpful. Additionally, it's just possible that you, in your capacity as Mr. Climer's security team, would look like imbeciles. Nobody wants that on their permanent record. So. Does anybody have a problem with how I handled things?"

Both men shook their heads.

Boyd said, "Say it."

"No problem," they said together, overlapping just a little.

"Good," I said. "Because a case could be made that I didn't have to kill those men to prevent this kidnapping. And that would make you accomplices, if what I did were considered a crime. Do you understand?"

Nods.

Boyd said, "Say it."

"Understood," they overlapped.

"Excellent." I turned to Climer. "I'm going to leave these gentlemen with you, to look out for you. How is Miss Crosby?"

"Still out like a light," Climer said, "last time I checked. When those two were haulin' me out of the bedroom like a bale of hay, Mavis was snorin' her fool ass off."

"Well, there's no reason to tell her anything," I said. "She doesn't need to know she was drugged. She doesn't need to know you were grabbed. Tonight never happened." I turned to the security guys. "Right, gentlemen?"

"Never happened," they said.

"Now, my friend and I have things to deal with back in town. Everyone going to be all right? Anything anybody needs? No? Good."

Outside, Boyd grabbed my arm. "We really should get rid of them."

"What, and Climer, too, I suppose?"

"Not Climer. Broker wouldn't like that. But those other goofs."

I shook my head. "I don't think so. Anyway, I don't go around killing people willy-nilly. You know that."

Boyd sighed, nodded.

On the way back, the sun came up. The remaining trees had the same blazing colors as back home, reds, yellows, greens, browns.

I dropped Boyd off at the stakeout pad, then drove to the Highland Motel. Or I should say HIGH____ MOTEL. When I used the key in the door, and stepped into the darkened room, the silenced nine mil in hand, the girl didn't move, just lay there in obscene spread-legged distress. Well, not incredibly distressed, because she was sleeping. Snoring a little, if not snoring her fool ass off, as Climer had described his fiancée's visit to the Land of Nod.

I clicked on the bedside lamp and sat next to Brandi.

She blinked herself awake and looked over at me. I have never seen a more mingled expression of fear and hope in my life.

"What happened?" she asked, softly. She often played the little-girl sex card, but right now she really did sound like a little girl.

"Did you know that kidnapping is a capital crime?"

"What's a capital crime?"

"It's where they execute you. Electric chair in this state, I believe. Strap you in, throw the switch."

"I didn't kidnap nobody."

"You were in on it. How close were you to Bruno?"

"Not close. That sounds like something happened to him."

"How close?"

"Well, I fucked him once. Took him about two seconds. That's about it. First I met him was at the club, just last week."

"And Eddie?"

"Hardly knew him. Just a pal of Bruno's. Did something bad happen to Bruno?"

"I killed him."

She swallowed. "Oh. And Eddie?"

I nodded. "How do you feel about Larry?"

She was thinking about crying. "Same as Eddie. Just some guy. You're just trying to scare me."

"Do you know what felony murder is?"

"Does it mean that murder is…a felony?"

"It means that if somebody gets killed, no matter who does the killing, during the commission of a crime…of a *felony* crime…everybody in on that crime is guilty of murder."

"I never murdered nobody!"

"The three I killed tonight, you're as guilty of that as me. Electric-chair guilty, Brandi. Or would you prefer Wanda on your headstone?"

"I don't want a fucking headstone!"

"Good girl. Because I don't want to put you under one. I haven't told Max Climer about your role in this. As far as I'm concerned, you helped me out last night so I could prevent that kidnapping."

She nodded. "Yes, I'm your helper."

My helper who was on her back handcuffed and strapped naked to a cheap-motel-room bed.

"You have one more night at the Climax Club," I said.

"I do if you let me up, and don't...do anything to me."

"Here's what *you're* going to do, Brandi. You're going to finish out your engagement at the club. You're going to be a happy little stripper and, if you see him, you'll thank Max Climer for the opportunity, and say that you hope to come back. Okay?"

She was nodding. "Okay."

"None of this ever happened."

"None never happened."

"You talk about this to anybody, you'll put me in an untenable position."

"I won't talk to nobody. Put you in a un-what?"

"A bad place. A position where I have to do something I don't want to do."

"Like kill me."

"Like kill you. Neither of us wants that."

"No. No, we sure don't."

I undid the handcuffs and dropped them in the left pocket of my windbreaker. Unstrapped her wrist and ankle that had been bound with torn pillowcase. She immediately flung herself at me and hugged me, hugged me hard.

"Thank you," she said. "Thank you."

I hugged her back. Somewhere in there was a sweet kid.

She backed away a little and said, "You wanna...do something? Like to seal the deal?"

"No. No, thank you."

"Wait a second," she said.

She ran to the bathroom and sat and tinkled, leaving the door open, giving me an embarrassed little grin. When she was done, she washed her hands and brushed her teeth, then emerged, still naked, and extended her hands in *tah-dah* fashion. "Fresh as a daisy. You sure you don't wanna? Last chance!"

"No, really. I've had a busy evening."

She came over and hugged me again. Looked up and said, "You did me a big favor. And I don't just mean letting me stay alive and all. I mean…I learned a lesson. I learned there's lines you shouldn't cross."

I smiled, nodded, slipped out of her grasp. She gave me the little-girl wiggle-finger wave as I went out.

I paused on the second-floor walkway, leaned against the wrought-iron rail. Sighed, smiled to myself. It wasn't every day I guided a kid like her onto the straight and narrow path.

But good as that felt, I was still left with a bitter reality—that failed kidnapping was just a sideshow. Somewhere out there a couple of lowlifes were preparing to kill Max Climer.

And so was whoever hired them.

ELEVEN

The Corner Newsstand on South Highland took up a corner, all right, but wasn't a newsstand in the traditional sense—this was one of those long, narrow book, magazine and tobacco shops, with the latter commodity lending a pungent aroma throughout.

Late on a Saturday morning—I'd grabbed a few hours sleep since our rescue efforts last night—business was good, making navigating around other browsers a real trick. On either side of the shop were magazine racks, with news, entertainment and women's subjects on the right side, and men's-themed material, from sports to skin mags, on the left. In between were aisles of double-sided bookcases of hardcovers and mostly paperbacks.

I selected a L'Amour, *Ride the Dark Trail*, and paid for it up front. The indifferent college girl at the counter, reading a well-thumbed *Feminine Mystique* paperback, peered at me from behind big black-rimmed glasses, her dark hair hanging like steady rain, slanted shelves of cigars in boxes framing her, and informed me that the manager, Mr. Peck, was in back.

She wasn't lying—a door that said, LEONARD PECK, MANAGER, PLEASE KNOCK, awaited me at the far end of this wide-ranging literary world that included authors from Marcel Proust and Charles Dickens to Jacqueline Susann and Agatha Christie, and periodicals ranging from *U.S. News & World Report* and *Sports Illustrated* to *Better Homes and Gardens* and *Juggs*.

My knock got me a cheerful, "Come in please," from behind the door, which I opened and went in.

The office was small, and so was the man behind the large

metal desk that took up much of the space. His dark hair was receding a little with some salt in the pepper; his eyes were the same very dark brown as his thick mustache, his face oval, wide nose, modest mouth. He was in a short-sleeved white shirt with a navy bow tie that matched his suspenders.

"Leonard Peck," he said pleasantly, but not rising or offering a hand. "May I help you?"

The wall behind him was arrayed with framed civic and business awards, lots of calligraphy and gold medal-type seals. The desk was piled with neat stacks of papers and files, plus family photos and a phone and pen holder and blotter and a triangular wooden name plate that said, you guessed it, LEONARD PECK, MANAGER. Typewriter on a stand. Two file cabinets. A visitor's chair.

Before taking the latter, I said, "Mr. Peck, my name is Jack Quarry. I wonder if you might spare me a moment."

"May I ask what your business is?"

"I'm a security consultant. Doing a job for Max Climer, down the street."

This news did not impact his pleasantness. He gestured to the visitor's chair, still smiling. "Please sit, Mr. Quarry."

I did. "I understand, sir, that you're part of a citizen's group that objects to Mr. Climer doing business on your...turf?"

He started nodding halfway through that. His chair was a high-back swivel number that made him look like the king of his little kingdom. "That's true in a sense, Mr. Quarry. As far as it goes."

"How far would that be? I noticed, for example, that you carry *Climax Magazine* and a number of other pretty explicit men's magazines."

He nodded, the smile never leaving. "We do. I share with Mr. Climer an enthusiasm for the First Amendment. I am happy to sell my customers whatever reading material might interest them."

"Well, that confuses me, Mr. Peck. Hasn't your group made its opposition to Mr. Climer's business painfully clear? Haven't you made efforts to have city ordinances introduced to hamper or block his activities?"

The smile continued, as did his patience. "Mister…Quarry, was it? Mr. Quarry, the Highland Strip Merchants Association is concerned with improving the reputation of this area. We have a business district that is coming back rather successfully after a dismal period. Are you familiar with what this area had become?"

"I'm not local, but I understand it was considered the heart of the Memphis drug scene."

"Heroin, cocaine, morphine, PCP, barbiturates and amphetamines, LSD, mescaline and of course marijuana, sold openly. Well, of course it led to police raids, and then riots, when the students who frequented the area felt they were being invaded for no good reason."

What it is ain't exactly clear.

"Eventually shops that were fronts for drug-selling were closed down, by which time many legitimate businesses had already been driven out. The Strip became…'uncool.' For several years, we were a ghost town. And now the area is fighting back."

"And you see Max Climer as a threat to that."

He raised a gentle hand. "We…or at least *I*…have no objection to his publishing business. It's somewhat disconcerting that much of his photography is conducted on those premises, but…out of sight, out of mind. The problem is the Climax Club. It's a hotbed of prostitution and illegal drugs."

I shifted in the metal chair. "Mr. Peck, the Climax Club is no

wide-open dope-selling operation. And if there's any prostitution going on, the management isn't part of it. They may
look the other way, when a dancer 'dates' a patron after hours,
but…"

"Even if I grant you that," Peck said, finally frowning, "pre-
senting as it does 'exotic dancing,' the Climax Club sends a very
wrong signal to a city just coming to accept an improved Highland Strip."

"The members of your association—just how deep does
their animosity toward Max Climer go?"

"I don't understand, sir."

"I'm looking into anonymous death threats."

He sighed, shook his head. "Well, that's to be expected, with
an iconoclast like Mr. Climer. But retailers, merchants, aren't
likely to stoop to that level. We're honest businessmen, not…
hoodlums."

"Sometimes honest businessmen do business with hoodlums,
though."

And another frown. "What are you implying?"

"You own and operate two adult bookstores elsewhere in the
city. The sort of hardcore pornography sold in those kinds of
shops is often generated by organized crime."

The smile returned, but it was no longer pleasant or friendly.
"I am the largest distributor of books and magazines in a three-
state area, Mr. Quarry. I distribute to my own and to other
stores, and my holdings include half a dozen adult bookstores,
in those three states. My enterprises are in *no* way criminal."

I shrugged. "It's just that old saying about lying down with
dogs and getting up with fleas…if you are dealing with the kind
of people who generate hardcore pornography, you might be in
a position to have somebody, well…taken care of."

His face became the blank thing he hung his smiles on.

"This conversation, Mr. Quarry, has taken an unpleasant turn. And if I may say so, an unnecessary one."

"How so?"

"I understand that Max Climer is seriously contemplating moving his operation elsewhere—his publishing to bigger, more modern quarters, and the Climax Club to a more appropriate area out on Winchester Road."

"In which case you'd have no gripe with him."

"No. Quite the opposite."

"How's that?"

And now the smile returned. "We sell a lot of copies of *Climax Magazine* at our various locations, Mr. Quarry. Now, if you'll excuse me, I'm trying to get some work done so that I might have the rest of the day with my family."

In Germantown, the high-income area just east of Memphis, with its public parks, planned neighborhoods and low crime rate, I tooled the Mustang convertible through winding suburban streets with colonial and farmhouse-style homes until, on Scarlet Road, I came to the future home of the editor and publisher of *Climax Magazine*. I was not alone, by the way.

Obviously one of the newer mansions in the area, its single sprawling floor was a ranch-style gone mad, white brick with black roof trim, square windows and a bright pink front door. It looked like the most expensive trailer in the world. I left the Mustang on the circular redbrick drive where the pink Caddy and several sporty cars were parked, and advanced hand-in-hand with my date to the pink door.

Max Climer had left word at the club for me to join him here this afternoon. He wanted to show off the new digs. I could bring a guest if I wanted to.

Leon, the bartender who gave me the message, said, "Mr.

Climer says he figures you made some friends while you were in town," meaning the strippers. Well, I didn't feel like asking Brandi. I'd thought about inviting that redheaded waitress, Sally, but instead had a wicked little notion, and invited Climer's niece, Corrie Colman, instead.

She had jumped at the chance to see what kind of "hedonistic indulgence" her uncle was about to immerse himself in, but I had warned her on the way over, "Chances are he and Mavis are throwing an orgy or something. But don't worry."

"Oh?" she'd asked, not make-up-free this afternoon, the pouty mouth all glossy red, the big brown eyes framed in light green shadow.

"I'll corner the market on you myself."

She giggled at that, but didn't seem sure I was kidding. Neither was I.

So we stood together on the little porch with the big pink door in front of us and I rang the bell. Corrie was in a black tube top and flared jeans with a red floppy hat. If you care, I was in a gray polo and jeans. Mavis, who answered the door, was not in jeans. She was in a gold-chain bustier top through which her nipples poked and red-trimmed white panties that her pubic patch showed through, her dark hair up with a gold tiara and matching dangling earrings.

Corrie and I exchanged glances that said, *Orgy.*

"Come in, you two. Jack, who's your little friend?"

Corrie wasn't that little, particularly since she was in platform shoes. But Mavis was a tall drink of water. Water I wouldn't suggest drinking.

"We've met, actually," Corrie told her.

Nothing registered on the pretty yet horsey face.

"I'm Vernon's daughter. Cordelia?"

"Oh! The demonstrator!"

That made it sound like she went door to door with vacuum cleaners.

I said, "Where's Max?"

"Oh, he's somewhere. He said I should give you the tour."

And she did.

We entered a make-believe world of moiré wallpaper and draperies, gold crystal chandeliers, and terrazzo floors, dazzled and dazed as our barely dressed hostess casually flipped a hand here and flipped a hand there. Each room was dominated by a single color, like the formal green living room with an elaborate mint fireplace and a sunken area with a pair of shamrock-and-white curved couches on moss carpeting facing each other over an endless laurel-tinted glass coffee table, while in the background (adorning windows that looked out onto a swimming pool that was thoughtlessly blue) emerald drapes hung like sleek seaweed, the space extending into an equally leprechaun dining room.

Enjoying rare freedom from mono-color domination was a richly wood-paneled den with padded bar and a sectional couch not unlike mine at the A-frame, except that it sat ten and cost thousands of dollars; a massive coffee table edged with cushioning further extended seating.

Otherwise, there was a blue bedroom, and a yellow-and-orange one, and most of all a pink master bedroom with hot pink carpeting everywhere, a bubblegum-pink sea on which floated a massive raised flamingo-pink bed, while popping up like coral reefs here and there were pink-lemonade tinted French provincial furnishings, including a stand for the massive 26" TV.

Mavis was moving us through this museum of kitsch at a breakneck speed. Whether she was in the early minutes of a heroin high or if this were merely cocaine buzz, I was not expert enough to discern. But I knew that while she might be at her high point, her judgment wasn't—not when she took us down the hot-pink-carpeted hallway to the master bathroom.

Not that it wasn't impressive. It was as big as my living room at home, with a double vanity that was really quadruple, even if it only boasted a mere two sinks and twin mirrors. And the hot-pink carpeting was everywhere, including all around the sunken Jacuzzi in the middle of the room. That thing was big enough for six people to share, although right now there were only three in it.

The bubbling was on a low setting, otherwise we might have been warned that it was in use, and not interrupted the master of the house, who was appropriately naked as he took from behind an equally naked female who I recognized as the *Climax* Girl of the Month from a few months ago. I recognized her mostly from her slender curves, distinctive puffy nipples, and layered blonde hairstyle, because her face was buried between the thighs of another *Climax* Girl (feathered brown hair, voluptuous) from several months before that, who was lost in sexual reverie, seated on the edge of the hot tub, the bubbling of the Jacuzzi being loud enough, and the pink carpet thick enough, to make our entrance unannounced.

Climer looked a little silly, if lucky, baby-faced, blank-eyed, with a small pot belly only half-hidden by the water and black Caesar curls clinging wetly to his forehead, giving them a rather pubic look. Several small mirrors with the ghosts of cocaine lines were on the edges of the hot tub like invitations to the party.

All I could do was think, *I killed three guys last night so you could go on playing baby Caligula?*

"Oh, sorry, honey," Mavis told him.

Climer stopped humping, which caused the muff-diver to come up for air, wondering what was up, or what wasn't up.

"Jesus, Quarry," Climer said, aghast. "You brought my *niece*?"

I shrugged. "How was I supposed to know this is what you'd be up to?"

I mean, what were the odds it would be something like this? Not any more than eighty percent, right? Ninety?

As for Corrie, I had to hand it to her. She just shook her head and smirked at him, and said, "You finish up, unc. We'll wait for you in the den."

To give Climer and his girls credit, they got right back into the game. Not everybody can get the mood happening again in a situation like that.

Mavis led us to the den, where she pointed me to the well-stocked shelf behind the bar and made an open-handed help-yourself gesture. Then she smiled enigmatically—or was that stupidly?—and whisked off.

I was behind the bar with Corrie, still in her floppy red hat, on the other side, like a customer. "Where's she off to?" she asked, making a face.

"I don't know," I said. "Maybe to get into something more comfortable."

"More comfortable than next-to-nothing?"

"That was a joke. You need to get used to my jokes."

She smirked. "I think I'm starting to. You knew something like this would happen, when you invited me along, didn't you?"

"I didn't know. Exactly. Hey, I've always had an ornery streak. What can I get you?" I had found a can of Coke in a little refrigerator back here and was pouring it into a glass of ice cubes. "There's beer. 7-Up. Wine."

She ordered a glass of Chardonnay and I gave it to her. She

went over and deposited herself on the endless couch and I joined her.

"He's a terrible man, my uncle," she said.

"You said you always liked him. And you're drinking his wine, aren't you?"

"He's an embarrassment. Look around at this idiotic place. It's the kind of life some Arab sheik thinks is badass. Or some actor who makes it suddenly rich. It's all terrible taste and vulgar excess. Think what somebody *responsible* could do with this kind of wealth!"

I sipped Coke, shrugged. "Why don't you try to put him on the right path?"

Her eyes got big under the brim of the red hat. "What? Are you fucking kidding me?"

"No. Strikes me he's been pretty successful. He's not just some poor white trash who won the lottery—he built this himself, for good or ill. He's got a real knack for putting out a magazine."

"What, 'Dickhead of the Month'?"

"Exactly. That's political satire. He's getting farther with it than a bunch of college girls picketing a strip club."

I'd gone too far. She didn't like that at all. She set down her glass of wine on the coffee table, which was no larger than New Jersey, and said, "I'd like you to take me home. *Right now.* This place makes me sick."

"Do I make you sick?"

"Why don't you get me out of here before you do?"

So, doing my best to remember the layout of the place, I walked her to the front door and we were just about to step outside when suddenly Max Climer was there, in another silk robe (burgundy), his hair still damp, his expression contrite.

"This was my fault," he said.

"Corrie needs to go home," I said. "Female trouble."

She gave me a look.

"Take her," he said, "but come back. We need to talk business. About last night, and, just…business."

"All right."

It was late afternoon now. On the way to her apartment at the Claridge House, Corrie didn't speak at first, the pouty mouth doing its thing.

I said, "Come on now. We both knew what we were getting into this afternoon. You thought it would be a hoot, didn't you? And so did I."

She smiled, and then she laughed. "Why don't you feed a girl first, before you drop her off and go back to the orgy?"

I said okay and she guided me to a funky place called Ray Gammon's. The menu bragged of home-cooked meals, and I said I had my doubts that Ray Gammon, whoever he was, lived in the kitchen.

"You're right," she said. "He died recently. A famous golf pro around here."

"Oh. Bad joke."

"No, they're closing down soon and I thought you might get a kick out of the joint. Best catfish around."

The meal was great and the conversation even better. She wasn't mad at me anymore. So of course I started teasing her again.

I asked her what she was majoring in, and she said, "English, with a minor in philosophy."

"Wow. Two ways not to get a job."

She took that well, then got reflective. "Maybe what's really going on with me is I'm jealous of my uncle and even my dad."

"Well, maybe I can find us a hotel with a Jacuzzi."

She smirked. "No, I mean…here I am all up-in-arms about

social issues and, like you rightly say, my money-hungry, sex-addicted uncle, with the help of my business-oriented daddy, is the one getting his political views out there. It galls me that he's making social change, and doing it on the backs of women!"

"Usually it's the women on their backs."

That made her laugh. She didn't want it to, but it did. "You know, Jack, I like having you around. You sort of…keep me honest."

"Somebody has to."

"How long will you be working for my uncle?"

"Not sure. Probably not much longer."

"Oh. That's kind of too bad."

By the time we were back in the Mustang, night had fallen and frogs were talking to each other and insects singing their own song. This was the south, all right. I leaned over and kissed her. It was soft and it was sweet. Maybe it didn't top fucking the *Climax* Girl of the Month in the ass, but it was all right.

When I pulled up in front of the Claridge House, she gave me a kiss, a nice long one, and said, "You wanna come up?"

"I should get back to that X-rated episode of the *Beverly Hillbillies*. What are you doing tomorrow?"

"Maybe studying. Nothing else—it's Sunday."

"Well, I meant after church, of course."

She got out of the car, laughing, then leaned in like a carhop and said, "You know where to find me," and ran off.

This time it was Climer who answered the bell by the big pink door. He was still in his burgundy silk robe, smoking a cigarette now.

"Thanks for comin' back," he said. Then the small smile in the bland baby face got accompanied by a twinkle in his eyes. Yes, a goddamn twinkle. He asked, "Did you bang my little niece?…No. Sorry. None of my business. Bad taste."

Yes, Max Climer was worried that he might have wandered into the realm of bad taste.

He walked me back to the den where Corrie's mostly untouched glass of white wine was still on the massive coffee table. He got behind the bar and asked, "Beer? Hard stuff?"

"Coors or anything but Budweiser."

He grinned at me, cigarette dangling. "You have no taste, Quarry."

Taste again.

He brought me a Coors and a Bud for himself and settled in next to me on the couch, not too close, since there was plenty of room.

He said, "I figured we should talk about last night."

"We're not going to talk about last night, Max, because last night never happened. Anyway, it was really morning. The wee hours."

"Okay." He let out smoke. "What about repercussions?"

I sighed. "Well, you'll likely hear from the cops. I haven't seen the news, or an evening paper, but that van with the three dead dipshits in it will likely be written off as an organized crime hit of some kind. Eventually, though, that trio will be linked to you. They worked for you."

His arm was along the back of the couch, his feet crossed and resting on the coffee table. "Recent hires. Not on the books yet."

"Well, if nobody comes around asking, so much the better. If they do, don't try to fake it. Say they were recent help and admit you don't check references on bodyguards and so on. At some point you may be asked about me."

"What do I say?"

"That I claimed to be a security expert, and gave you an off-the-cuff assessment of your security situation and you were convinced. Plus, I said I was a Vietnam vet and war hero."

He was studying me with those rarely blinking eyes. "Listen… do you have a background that would hold up on examination? You know, if I wanted to hire you full-time?"

"I do. The Vietnam service is real. The Bronze Star, too. But I'm not looking for a job. I already *have* a job, as you know."

"And I'm guessing it pays well."

"It does."

"What if I were to double it?"

"No sale. No offense, but…not interested."

His tone got softly chummy. "There's not just money available, Quarry. There's more pussy than you can shake a stick at. There's nose candy and other recreational stuff, as long as you stay away from anything hard."

"Your bartender, the black dude? Leon? He's the one providing grass and coke to the girls, right?"

He frowned. "Right. You spotted that?"

"Yeah, and without a seeing-eye dog. Be careful, Max. Be more careful."

Grinning, he stabbed out his cigarette in an ashtray on the coffee table. "That's just the kind of service you could lend me. Come work with me, Quarry. I mean, now that the job here is done."

I frowned. "What do you mean, 'done'?"

He gave me the world's tiniest shit-eating grin. "Well…last night…which never happened…that was *it*, right? That was the threat, and you squashed it?"

I shook my head. "No. That was something else. Something that reflects in general what a target you are, but had nothing to do with the contract we discussed. I'm still working on that."

The unused-looking face turned blister white. "I'm still in the crosshairs?"

"Like a clay pigeon. At least one of the kill team is in town. Both should be soon. We'll take care of them. And I'm still looking into who hired them."

"Anything there?"

I shrugged. "I spoke to Leonard Peck. He seems like a respectable sort. But operating adult bookshops, that makes him a likely mob associate."

He let out some breath. "Hell. Okay. Well, I got faith in you, Quarry. I've seen how you handle things."

"Thanks."

He hauled his feet off the coffee table and rose and said, "Come with me a second."

I nodded and got up, followed him, and before we knew it, we were back in the master bathroom. In the sunken whirlpool, his fiancée Mavis, as naked as when she was at the end of her strip act, was sucking on one of the much more real tits of yet another *Climax* centerfold, a blonde. Mavis had her hand underwater and was doing something to the blonde, who seemed to like it.

"Two of them, two of us," Climer said, with a baby-tooth leer. "Just drop your drawers and we can climb in there with 'em."

"No thanks," I said. "I never learned to swim."

Of course I swam just fine—but so did the germs and sperms swimming around in there.

Giving the sales pitch one more try, Mavis got herself up on the edge of the hot tub, spread her legs and invited the blonde's attention. That's when I noticed skin-colored make-up on her inner thighs getting washed away, exposing needle marks and bruising.

Time to go.

I was in the Mustang, with the engine started, when Climer

in his silk robe came to the door and called, *"Quarry!* Phone for you!"

I went back in and was led to a phone in the hall.

"Quarry," Boyd's voice said. Phone booth. I could hear street sounds. "The shooter's in town, and they're both on the move."

TWELVE

"I'll be in a joint called Lafayette's," Boyd's voice said. "In Overton Square—you know where that is?"

I did. I'd been there earlier, because Corrie's apartment building ran along an edge of it, and that burger joint we'd eaten at, Huey's, was in the thick of it.

Overton Square was everything the Highland Strip might have been, if the druggies hadn't moved in. It was counterculture at its most benign, a Southern-fried Greenwich Village, home to maybe a dozen restaurants and twice as many trendy shops.

Saturday night, Overton would be hopping.

"Should I check out their stakeout," I said, "and make sure they're who we think they are?"

"They're who we think they are," Boyd said. "Heading into the can, I brushed up against the one who just showed up, and he was packing. And don't say, 'Maybe he was just happy to see you.'"

"Could be an undercover cop."

"No. This is *them*, Quarry. But, uh, I…never mind."

"What?"

"Tell you when you get here." He gave me the address and hung up.

Wonder what that's about, I thought.

The evening cool enough to keep me in the windbreaker, I left the Mustang in a public parking lot a block or so from Lafayette's Music Room, a two-story joint twice as wide as the TGI Friday's next door. Two marquee pillars bookended four double-door entrances with four large arched windows above, all with Bourbon Street trimmings. The act playing was BIG STAR, with "REUNION!" below. So apparently a band I'd never heard of was getting back together, for one night anyway.

My excitement contained, I paid the two-buck cover, moving past posters of previous attractions (Billy Joel, Barry Manilow, Phoebe Snow, Pure Prairie League, Linda Ronstadt) and found myself in a big packed smoky room with college kids and other under-thirties at little tables with not much room for dancing, balconies on either side similarly full. The audience had a date-night look, lots of guys in paisley or striped shirts and girls in mini-dresses or new bell jeans. Up on the stage, the band was similarly attired, maybe a little sloppier. They were playing some song I'd never heard before, but generally seemed like just another garage band. The crowd loved them, though.

That crowd was frustrating me, because as I edged through the standing room at back, I had trouble spotting Boyd. But he spotted me and waved and that finally did the trick. He was upstairs, at a little table for two, looking a tad old for this crowd but fitting in well enough, in a light blue leisure suit with pink-and-white-and-blue paisley shirt.

I made my way up a tight winding stairway and squeezed through young bodies to his table, where he sat before a mostly empty beer pilsner.

"They still here I hope?" I asked.

"They're here," Boyd said, and gave a slight nod directly across from him, on the opposite balcony.

It was a little like looking in a mirror. One guy was five or ten years older than the other one, who was about my age, average-looking, the black sheep of the Brady Bunch. The older one had Boyd's head of curly brown hair, but no mustache and more angles in his face, like a cigar store Indian with a white man's Afro. My counterpart was in a polo and jeans, though his shirt was red (I would never call attention to myself that way) and Boyd's near-doppelganger was in a denim leisure suit with a black shirt exploding with pink flowers—orchids, I'd guess, but from here I wasn't sure.

"Why would they pick a place like this," Boyd asked, noticeably tense, "for their first meet? How do you go over stakeout intel in a crowded noisy hole like this?"

The Lafayette was certainly no hole, or if so was a very big and deep one, but the remark only demonstrated that Boyd was on edge. Something really was eating at him.

"It's not how *we* do it," I said, "but on the other hand, you can get lost in a crowd. And who's listening to their conversation but themselves, when the band is on?"

Big Star were doing a song about a slut right now. Or anyway the word "slut" was in it a lot.

"No," Boyd said, "they aren't here on business."

We had long ago learned to speak in noisy places without yelling at each other. We both had the lip-reading skills that helped that effort.

"What do you mean?"

He said, "Don't you see? Don't you get it?"

"See what? Get what?"

"They're a couple!"

I almost said "couple of what?" Then the older guy put a hand on the other's shoulder and whispered in his ear. It did look like kind of intimate.

"So what if they're a couple," I said, shrugging. "You got something against two men having a loving relationship?"

He scowled at me in a way he never had in all our years. "It just bothers me. Do I have to explain it? It doesn't *feel* right."

"They're not gay."

"*You're* the expert?"

"Okay," I said, shrugging, getting why he was bothered. "It makes you queasy, maybe I can handle it alone."

"Don't patronize me, Quarry!"

"I'm not. I wasn't."

"We'll do this together."

"Fine."

"I'm just…*weirded* out, that's all."

I shrugged, doled out half a smirk. "Well, just cool it. This place is too packed for us to do anything about them, anyway."

"I think they're just out enjoying themselves."

I still didn't think those two were necessarily gay, not that I gave a shit either way.

But I said, "Sure. We'll find a better time and place. Still, we'll stick with them tonight, okay?"

Boyd nodded. He was frowning. Way off his feed. "Okay."

The band did several more songs. One called "When My Baby's Beside Me" won me over. They took a break and a number of people left their tables, including the intimate pair across from us.

We did, too.

They pushed through the crowd toward an exit. Lots of the kids were going out for some fresh air and to pollute that air with cigarette smoke, not that they weren't leaving plenty behind. Few wandered off, however—these were just audience members stretching their legs, waiting for the next set by a local-favorite band. But our doppelgangers broke from the herd and ambled down the street.

The walk along Madison to the nondescript-looking little bar called George's took only a couple of minutes. The two men up ahead of us walked side by side, but not terribly close. They certainly didn't hold hands or in any other way express anything like affection. Just two guys out looking for a little action. Female action.

"Not gay," I whispered to Boyd, as the pair entered the bar. "Not that it matters. But they're not. So just lighten up, buddy."

"Okay, Quarry. Okay."

I opened the door for Boyd and noticed the logo on the glass: GEORGE'S TRUCK STOP AND DRAG BAR.

It wasn't only men in the place—there were women, too. But the men were with men, and the women with women, and this was a showbar full of glitter and sequins, with disco lights and a mirrored revolving ball over a raised dance floor with flashing yellow, red and green lighted-under square tiles on which same sex couples danced, some in attire no different than any disco, others in full-on drag. Right now "Boogie Down" was playing, very loud.

Yep, I thought to myself. Memphis—home of the blues and rock 'n' roll.

The place was hopping, but not swarming like the nearby Lafayette's. We had no trouble getting a table for two along the dance floor. Our counterparts were just two tables away from us, near the elevated DJ booth. In some ways the place reminded me of the Climax Bar. But I doubted the likes of Brandi Wyne would be stripping here, nor would any miner's helmets be rented out.

I ordered a Coke and Boyd got a daiquiri. I was keeping as close an eye on my partner as we both were on our targets. I was determined that daiquiri would be his final drink of the night—he'd already had at least one beer at Lafayette's.

"The young guy is the shooter," I said.

Boyd nodded. "I saw him pull up outside the pawnshop building. The other guy greeted him. Gave him a hug…if you were still wondering if they were queer or not. The kid was lugging a leather rifle case. A Kolpin, I'd say."

"Right out in the open?"

A little shrug. "Didn't look suspicious, not with a pawnshop right handy. He had a khaki duffel, too. Like to know what handguns are in there. Think he's too young for Vietnam?"

"No." I'd stolen a decent look at his face and it had that cold hardness some people got over there.

"Lady Marmalade" was driving them crazy out on the dance floor. If those boas were real and not feathers, we'd be deep in the jungle about now.

"Listen," I said, leaning close, "this dive is a better option than Lafayette's."

"Better option how?"

"Not as crowded."

"It's crowded enough."

"Not really, not wall-to-wall like up the street. If we could get them alone, the restroom maybe, or a back room or something, we'd have them cold."

Boyd gave me a patronizing glance. "You really think the men's room is going to be empty at any moment in this establishment? Between getting rid of drinks standing up and blowjobs sitting down, it'll be busier in there than on the dance floor."

"Okay, a back room, then."

"Oh, really? You and I just go over there and suggest a foursome, maybe? You really want to waltz over there with me and come on to them, honey?"

"Don't do that." I told him a long time ago never to call me "honey." I felt about that the way Perry White did being called "chief" by Jimmy Olsen.

"Then don't insult my intelligence," he said. "And don't assume all gays are sex maniacs eager to try anything as long as it isn't straight."

The drinks came. We sat and drank them slowly. He was even better at pouting than Corrie. On the dance floor nearby, our twins were dancing slow, embracing each other to Barry White—"Can't Get Enough of Your Love, Babe."

It was unsettling.

Maybe I did have something against gays after all. Or maybe seeing two men dancing romantically who I was trying to figure out how to kill was working at me a little.

"Boyd," I said, "we have to figure out a way to deal with them *now*…tonight…when we have them together and away from that stakeout pad."

"What's wrong with taking them out in that apartment? They won't be expecting it."

"What, and leave two bodies across the street from the Climax Club? You think the Broker will appreciate our leaving Climer in that kind of mess?"

"I guess not…"

"Or maybe we just go clomping up there, past the tenant on the second floor, take care of business, and wrap the results up in plastic sheeting, and then what? Haul them down the stairs, one at a time, like mummies? Shove one in my trunk, another in yours? And then go off driving around looking for another back road to decorate?"

KC and the Sunshine Band's "That's The Way I Like It" had our two reflections back out on the dance floor, getting down. That was worse than the slow dancing.

"Look," I said, leaning in again, "this is the perfect place. In this setting, a couple of dead fags, pardon my French, will be shrugged off by the cops in a very helpful way. Hell, the owners of this joint will probably dispose of the bodies *for* us, to fight the bad publicity. We should take advantage."

"The shitter," Boyd said defensively, "and your imaginary

back-room trysting spot, are Oh-you-tee out. And so is this place, unless you have another, better idea."

"Well...I have a silencer in one windbreaker pocket and a nine mil in the other. The next loud disco song, I just walk up behind them at their table, pop them, one two, and go on my merry way. You can wait outside for me."

The smile under the bristly mustache was as wide as it was snide. "Listen to yourself, Quarry. You stand behind them and let go with a noise-suppressed, big-ass automatic, and you figure the convulsions the bodies make won't give you away? And that the bark of the gun, even neutered, will be lost to people sitting nearby? Give me a goddamn fucking break."

He had a point. Two points, actually.

And my idea would have got tabled anyway, because the disco music stopped and the floor show began. On a small platform stage past the lighted-up dance floor was a piano, Hammond organ, drum kit, stand-up microphone and a Day-Glo painted palm tree. An individual introducing him/herself as Marilyn Misfit, in the Monroe *Bus Stop* outfit (brave by any sex), introduced one drag act after another. Bette Davis did a monologue of her most famous movie lines to piano and rim-shot accompaniment. Judy Garland sang "Over the Rainbow" (quite moving, actually) to Hammond orchestration, and three other appropriately attired and made-up performers did lip-sync pantomime to records by Cher, Barbra Streisand and Marlene Dietrich, played by the DJ over the house sound system.

During Marlene's "Falling Love Again," a few tables emptied—it was an overly campy performance, I guess, or maybe just too easy a choice. Anyway, our two friends were among those who appeared bored as they got up and headed out. I felt kind of bad for the performer.

Boyd looked at me, eyebrows lifting, and I nodded. We didn't know where they were going, but we were going there, too.

Out in the cool evening, with a few drinks under their belts, our friends were nice and loose as they walked down the street, the older one with an arm around the younger guy's shoulder for a while. Then they were hand in hand, and finally they stole a kiss. I admit it made me uncomfortable, but I don't think it had anything to do with homosexuals creeping me out.

Why the hell was I feeling, what, *sorry* for these lowlifes? And you shouldn't, either. So they liked each other. So they were capable of affection. Keep in mind what they did for a living. These two were stone-cold killers, and had almost certainly earned what was coming to them, many times over.

They crossed to the packed parking lot, no attendant on duty, and nobody else heading for a vehicle. This was the same lot my Mustang was parked in. That was lucky.

"What are they driving?" I asked Boyd, sotto voce.

"It's an aqua Marlin, probably around '67, '68."

A cheap-ass car but a fun ride. Kind of thing I would pick up at a sleazy used car dealership at the start of a gig. Made sense.

I spotted the AMC would-be sports car toward the back of the fenced-in area, an alley beyond. Boyd and I slowed, keeping an easy stride.

"Follow my lead," I said, and ambled toward the Mustang, parked half a row down from the Marlin.

"What?" Boyd asked, soft.

"Just get in," I said.

I climbed behind the wheel of the convertible, its top up, Boyd slid in on the passenger side, and I started up the car.

"Glove compartment," I said.

Boyd got in there, found the spare silenced nine mil waiting. He took it, draped it in his lap.

We rolled toward where they were getting into the Marlin, the young guy opening the driver's door, older guy the rider's one. Neither was in yet when I slowed to a stop and got out, wearing a big smile.

"You guys know where Godfather's is?" I asked, walking over casually, my right arm alongside my leg, my hand hiding the nine mil behind me.

The older guy nodded and started pointing. He hadn't got any words out yet when I shoved the nose of the silenced weapon in his stomach and fired. The gun's cough was muffled further by his belly fat, and actually he made more noise himself, with a short grunt of pain, like a fist and not a slug had punched him. He dropped to his knees and I put one in his forehead, so he wouldn't have to suffer. Gut shots kill so fucking slow.

Meanwhile, Boyd had stepped out and taken a shot at the younger guy, from several feet. The kid had sensed something coming, and ducked out of the way, which gave the bullet a right rear window to puncture and spider-web. The kid must not have had a gun on him, because he rushed Boyd, who let go with one, two, three rounds, all body shots, kind of a panicky reaction, frankly, since a head shot would've stopped him.

But the kid tackled him and took him down, revealing three bloody gaping exit wounds, and when I got to them, Boyd was pinned under the dead kid, missionary position, and was screaming, "Get him off of me!"

"Shut up," I said, and did.

I glanced around, figuring somebody must have heard or seen something, but nobody was in sight and no sound of reaction could be heard. Directly across from us were boutiques, after hours, no clubs or restaurants, which was luck.

Boyd had some smears of blood on his shirt and suitcoat, but not drenched or anything. I helped him into the rider's side of the Mustang and we were out of there within seconds.

Back at the crash pad, I helped Boyd in and up the stairs like he was the one shot, not that dead kid back there. But my partner's legs were rubbery and he was moaning. Not crying, exactly, but close.

"Take a shower," I advised him, and he did.

I didn't have any blood on me or my clothes, but while Boyd was in the shower, I threw water on my face and brushed my teeth, generally trying to feel human again.

After the shower, Boyd got himself into some fresh clothes—another leisure suit, another paisley shirt—and said, "I don't think I could sleep. Too wired. Maybe could eat. Maybe."

I shrugged. "Let's try."

The restaurant announced itself as the oldest in Memphis, a tan brick building on the corner of South Main Street perched there like a ship's prow coming in, a green neon ARCADE riding a red neon RESTAURANT sign. It was so early we were damn near alone. But the sun was up.

We took an aqua-and-white booth and ordered breakfast from a pretty little brunette waitress in an aqua-and-white uniform—coffee and French toast for Boyd, coffee and eggs/bacon/hash browns for me. Orange juice for both.

"Jesus," Boyd said. "That was something."

"Something, all right."

"Did I fuck up, Quarry?"

Borderline.

"Not at all," I said.

"It just freaked me out. It was like we were killing ourselves."

"Not really."

"No?"

"No, we're partners but not lovers. I mean, when you fuck me in the ass, it's just a figure of speech."

He started to laugh. He laughed so hard he started crying. The waitress gave me a look as she delivered the food and I gave her back one that said, *Don't worry, he's fine.*

"And this job," Boyd said, just crying now, no laughter, "this goddamn job, it's not even finished."

"It's close to finished," I said.

"You think you know who hired those two?"

"Pretty good idea. Look, I'll handle this from here. All right? You've done your job, a lot more than your job. Nothing passive about the last two nights."

His expression was so earnest it hurt to look at. "You okay with that, Quarry? You're sure you're okay?"

"You bet. You clear out of here, as soon as you're up to it. Catch some sleep first, or get the first plane out and sleep there. I'll take it from here."

He smiled and seemed suddenly relaxed. "Thank you, Quarry."

"You bet, pal."

He dug into his breakfast and I dug into mine.

How many more jobs did this guy have left in him? I wondered.

THIRTEEN

The Sunday matinee at the Memphian Theater on Overton Square—a few minutes away from the Lafayette where last night's festivities had begun—was showing something called *The Rocky Horror Picture Show*. Apparently the grand old theater was a kind of art house now, and this oddball attraction might be expected to draw a sizeable college-age counterculture crowd.

But Corrie Colman and I were among the less than a dozen spectators who sat in stunned silence watching a drag queen right out of George's Truck Stop and Drag Bar try to seduce both halves of a young couple whose car had broken down at his/her spooky mansion in the rain. Of this select group, we were the only ones in the balcony, having sneaked past the CLOSED sign for some privacy.

Before the show started, we shared a small popcorn and sipped our respective Cokes and chatted.

"Just how tense are things between you and your father?" I asked her, knowing that nothing loosens up a date better and faster than asking her about her parents.

"Tense enough. I don't see him all that often. He lives in Collierville."

"Where's that?"

"Pricey suburb, past Germantown, and I don't get out there much. And you know where he *works*."

"You do drop by there from time to time," I reminded her. "With a few of your girlfriends."

She smiled a little at that, then shrugged. "He's too busy for me."

"Why's that?"

"The new woman in his life. Well, not *that* 'new'—it's been going on for a good six months. I'll *tell* you how close my father and I are—I haven't even *met* the woman. I don't even know who she *is*."

The previews came on. Something called *Female Trouble* with yet another drag queen was the next attraction. Either I was sensing a trend at the Memphian or, after last night, God was displaying the sick side of His sense of humor.

She was giggling over our popcorn.

"What?" I whispered.

She whispered back. "Reminds me of your bad joke yesterday."

"You'll have to be more specific."

" 'Female trouble'?"

"Oh."

She shifted in her seat a little. Still whispering, she said, "Listen, uh…reminds me. Female trouble is right. Time of the month, I mean. So we're kind of limited today. I mean, after the other night, you might expect…but I can't…some people *do*, some girls, but I never have, during my, you know…and…well, I'm sorry."

"We're in the balcony, aren't we? Maybe we'll think of something."

The movie was lively anyway, with some catchy rock 'n' roll. The drag queen had a familiar sneer, and maybe that's what prompted Corrie to lean over and say, "You know, this is Elvis' favorite theater."

He was a local boy.

I said, "No kidding?"

"Yeah. He rents it out and brings all his crew in to see his and other people's movies, and party. They go all night, I hear."

She was leaning very close, to share this crucial piece of Memphis history with me, and I kissed her on the mouth. No lip gloss today on those pouty (but not pouting) lips, just the ghost of butter topping. She kissed me back and her tongue tickled mine and we necked for a while. I put a hand on her tube top and traveled from one soft round mound to another and then tugged the top down and kissed her breasts, nuzzled her soft nipples till they got hard. I was getting hard, too. I wondered idly if the projectionist up there was enjoying the show.

"Touch-a, Touch-a, Touch-a Touch Me," a blonde on screen was singing.

When the song ended, Corrie, breathing hard, tugged her tube top back up rather discreetly and I thought that was the end of it. But instead she unzipped me and fished me out and began working me with her hand. Now and then she dipped down and put me in her mouth, just a little ways, kind of tentatively, clearly a girl who had limited experience in this area but was doing just fine for a beginner.

Or maybe she wasn't such a beginner, because I suddenly wondered if she hadn't planned this—I'd noticed her taking extra napkins when we bought our popcorn and now, as I reached my climax and her sweet little right hand pumped me, her left hand settled the rough couple of napkins on me and gently captured what we'd produced together.

I took it upon myself to put my dick back in my pants—she'd done enough for me already—and she was smiling at me impishly, ashamed and proud.

Then I put my arm around her and the movie got even dirtier.

❖

The Climax Club kept hours on Sunday identical to every other day of the week, opening at four P.M. But on Sunday the girls didn't go on till six, because business was slow. Not a table had a customer, with only a handful of blue-collar guys seated at the bar, watching football on the mounted TV, outnumbering the trio of bartenders.

It was about five. I'd dropped Corrie at her apartment house after another Huey's burger. I was in a dark blue polo and jeans, the little .25 in my windbreaker pocket.

I approached Leon, the shaved-headed bartender who looked like a slightly less muscular, unbearded Isaac Hayes.

"You got a minute, Leon?"

"Sure, Mr. Quarry. What you need?"

"Let's take a table."

"Sure. Bring along a couple beers?"

"Why not?"

He drew two pilsners of Coors and came around the bar. As always, he was in a white shirt, black bow tie and black trousers. I had taken a table across the room and in the far corner where, if a girl had been dancing, we'd have had the worst seat in the house. I wanted privacy, even with such a limited potential audience.

He set the beers down and we sat across from each other at the tiny table.

"Leon, you know what it is I've been doing around here."

He nodded and gave me that practiced, easygoing smile that got a bartender good tips.

"Sure do, Mr. Quarry, and I'm all in favor of what you been up to. This place bein' run *way* too loose and sloppy. Nice guy like Mr. Max? People can take advantage, bigtime."

"And I guess you'd know."

It was like I'd slapped him.

He said, "Pardon?" But the inflection was, *What the fuck?*

I had a sip of beer. Smiled easily. "You're aware that Mr. Climer…Max…doesn't see anything wrong with the girls here doing a little grass, occasional lines. And he seems to know you're the one providing the stuff, and I don't think he minds."

Leon was staring at me, his dark brown eyes cold and barely blinking now.

I went on: "What I don't think he knows is that you're providing his fiancée Mavis with smack."

He started to get up. "I think we done here."

My voice was calm and nearly a whisper. "No. We're just getting started. You're short a bartender, aren't you? And a bouncer? Maybe you've heard Max needs a new driver?"

He was taking that in with a frown, still standing there, half-turned to go; but not walking off.

"So what?" he said. "They quit. People quit."

"They didn't quit. I killed their asses. Sit down."

His eyes opened just a shade wider, and then he sat.

"They tried to kidnap 'Mr. Max,' and I'm giving you the benefit of the doubt that you weren't in on it."

"You best—"

"A friend of mine and I stopped the snatch from going down, and it got messy, but we cleaned it up. Probably in a day or two, you'll be questioned by the cops about the help who didn't show up on Saturday. You should get your story straight with Mr. Max, as soon as you can."

He said nothing, but a tightness around his eyes was pulsing.

I gave him a friendly smile. Took another sip of beer—he hadn't touched his.

"We all have our secrets, Leon. Me, I take care of security in my own way, and if you're wondering, Mr. Max approves. You have your secrets, too, like dealing smack to Mavis. But what I want to know is…why?"

His voice was a low rumble now. "Why what?"

"I've kept an eye on you. I don't think you're dealing smack to anybody but Mavis. Now I have my own notion about why that may be, so maybe the real question is…who?"

When a bald guy frowns, his whole forehead wrinkles. "*Who? Now* what the fuck are you—"

I raised a palm as if in court being sworn in. "Who was it that wanted you to deal that shit to Mavis? *Who*, Leon?"

He let air out from down around his toes; shifted in the seat. Made a show of shrugging. "Well, girl *wanted* it. What you think?"

"I think it wasn't your idea. That somebody told you to be her connection. Sure, she asked you, because you were giving her the softer stuff. It's natural. And I'm sure it wasn't hard for you to lay hands on what she wanted. But who were you doing that for? And if you say 'Mavis,' my next stop will be Max Climer, to tell him you're poisoning his sweetie."

His eyes and nostrils flared, like a rearing horse. "What is this, fuckin' blackmail?"

"No. It's a threat." I got very quiet and put some crazy in it. "I know you're a big guy. But you're not a killer. I took out somewhere between thirty and sixty little yellow bastards in Vietnam, and adding one big black bastard back home to the list won't lose me any sleep. *Who made you Mavis' connection, Leon?*"

He swallowed; his expression showed no fear, following my little rant, but a weariness had set in.

He said, "Mr. Climer—his deal all the way. I mean, not Mr. *Max* Climer, but…"

"Mr. Vernon Climer. Cousin Vernon."

The bartender nodded glumly. "Why the man wanted her on that stuff, I couldn't tell you."

"Guess."

"Well…she…she got a lot of sway over the *other* Mr. Climer. Mr. Max. She got ideas for the magazine. Was her idea to buy that fancy new house in Germantown. She wanted to star in movies Mr. Max Climer is plannin' to make, and she not somebody who looks good in front of a camera, believe you me. She kind of a hard, skanky-lookin' bitch."

"I noticed. But Max loves her. The heart wants what it wants."

"Don't it the fuck. But when she on the spike, Mavis, she easy to handle. She got one thing on her mind—just floatin' dreamy-like till next time, make it to the next high. All that ambition, out the window. Is my opinion. My observation."

"Okay, Leon. Thanks."

His eyebrows lifted. "That it?"

"Not quite. Who is the woman?"

Another endless forehead of frown. "Who is what woman?"

"The other day I needed to see Vernon, but he was in conference. When he finally came out, he looked like a sailor who just got back from shore leave. Who was the woman he was 'in conference' with?"

Leon cocked his head, narrowed his eyes. "You know, Mr. Quarry, that's the man's personal business."

He was willing to talk about Cousin Vernon paying him to keep Max's fiancée on H, but betraying sexual indiscretions? That was another thing entirely. A real breach of the understanding between men.

"Who, Leon? We've come this far."

He shrugged. "His cousin's wife. Dorrie. What's the harm? Mr. Max, he's divorcin' the bitch, ain't he? I mean, who cares?"

"Somebody does, or they wouldn't keep it secret."

He leaned in conspiratorially. "You ask me, it's some sick shit that defies human understandin'. They sneak around, keep the big affair a secret, then have sex back in his *office*? She does it all the time, man, she's here two, three times a week, goin' back there, like she gets a fuckin' *charge* out of screwin' ol' Vernon under Max's own roof. I mean, man, the marriage is *over*! Who *cares* who's bangin' who?"

"Leon, Max has been very generous to Dorrie. He's not made an enemy out of her, at least in his eyes. If he finds out she's having an affair with his cousin and business partner and best friend—who are all the same guy—it just might change his point of view. Toward both of them."

One eyebrow climbed the endless forehead. "Might just."

I sipped the Coors, nodded toward the back. "Speak of the devil, is Vernon here yet?"

"No, man, he don't come in on Sundays."

"Any idea where he is?"

He turned over a hand. "Sure. Cousin Vernon goes out to Mr. Max's cabin every Sunday afternoon and stays the night with, well, I guess you know who."

I had to laugh. "More of that banging the future ex-missus under her hubby's nose?"

"More of that, yeah. Not that she ain't worth screwin', for an old broad. But they's still one thing in this life I will never understand."

"What's that?"

"The mind of a fuckin' cracker."

As a Northern boy, I had no comment.

He gave me a look that asked if there was anything else, and I shook my head.

He was on his feet and just starting to head back to the bar, when I said, "Oh, Leon—is Max still out at stately Wayne Manor in Germantown?"

"No, he upstairs, in the penthouse," Leon said, and gestured with a thumb. "Came in a couple hours ago. Hauled Miss Mavis with him. She was *gone*, man."

"Well, she's going to have it worse before it gets better."

"Yeah, why that?"

"You're cutting her off."

He just thought about that for a moment, then shrugged, nodded and headed back behind the bar.

I had keys to the Yale locks separating the downstairs from the magazine office and penthouse above, and I used them.

As I had several days before, I came in through the kitchen, where as before a few empty Bud cans could be seen. I moved down the hall, past a partly open bedroom door that revealed Mavis zoned out on top of the big Victorian brass bed, covered with a blanket. It looked more like somebody in a coma than sleeping.

Max Climer was in the living room, a fresh Bud in hand, sunk down into one of the leather overstuffed chairs, looking only a little better than Mavis—not in a coma, but someone who just came out of one. He was in a purple-and-white track suit and trainers but had the puffy, slightly pudgy look of an individual who had never run farther than from the car to his house to get out of the rain.

The futuristic big-screen TV was on and a porn tape was playing, the sound down, a small blonde blowing John Holmes' monster dick, but though Climer's eyes were on the screen, he didn't really seem to be watching it.

Hearing me, he glanced my way as I settled into a similar nearby chair. "Quarry. Sneakin' up on me again. Glad *you're* not the one tryin' to get me."

I nodded toward the big screen. "Don't you ever get tired of sex?" Like I was anybody to talk.

"Rarely, but a guy does get jaded. Has to go for different

things, bigger things. That's what's so great about Mavis."

"What is?"

"She gets me. She knows monogamy isn't my thing, and she doesn't care. Doesn't fuckin' care. So…where are we? Am I still on the wrong end of the shootin' gallery?"

Him and Mavis both. Just different kinds of shooting galleries.

"I'm not going to tell you the details," I said. "But last night my partner and I took care of the two-man team sent to kill you."

He tried to process that. His small mouth became an "O" and his unblinking baby blues narrowed. "So where does that leave us?"

"It leaves us with whoever hired it still in the game, obviously. And I need to take them out before they hire somebody else and the fun starts all over again."

The unblinking eyes were droopy. "You said you'd been sniffin' around. Talkin' to people."

"I have. And I've ruled a lot of people out. That egotistical minister loves having you around to be his villain. Those women's libbers wouldn't hurt a fly, and would call the Humane Society if anybody did. That Highland Strip association guy sells *Climax Magazine* himself down the street. You're everybody's favorite asshole."

His smile was childish but rather winning. He raised the can of Bud. "Here's to me."

"I think I know who's behind this, Max, and I think I know how to confirm it. But first you have to be comfortable with it."

"Comfortable…?"

I told him.

"Jesus," he said, the eyes suddenly both not droopy and blinking like crazy. "You're *sure*? You're goddamn *sure*?"

I nodded. "I will be. You don't take this kind of step on a hunch. My question is…can you live with it?"

He sighed. Sipped his drink. Turned his eyes to the screen. "Will you look at the *size* of that thing! It's like that little gal is swallowin' an anaconda! You know, you can have all the money and success in the world, but only God can give you a cock like that."

There was something he could take up with Reverend Lesser Weaver. A theological discussion to find some common ground.

I sat forward and put some edge in my voice. "Max. Can you *live* with it? If you can't, you can take a chance and try to deal with this on a personal level, and maybe work things out, though I sure as hell don't think so…but if you do? I'll just go on to my next gig."

Eyes still on the screen, he said, "But will you look at the bad production! The lousy lighting! And the *acting*! Why do they try to do stories? When I get my video line going, it'll just be, you know, vignettes. Little situations that become big sex scenes!"

"Max. I need the go-ahead."

He swallowed hard and his gaze, unblinking again, turned itself on me. "Quarry…do what you think is right."

"Right isn't the word. Necessary is."

He swallowed. His lower lip was quivering. Was he trying not to cry?

"Do what's necessary," he said.

"Okay. Max?"

"Yes?"

"You surely realize that Mavis is back on the smack."

He swallowed. "I don't think so. She's just smokin' a little grass, doing a few lines…"

"Max. She's using. Get her some help or she'll be dead in a

few months, if you don't get caught up in a drug bust first that puts you out of business. I've already cut off her supply."

One blink. "You have?"

I nodded. "It's up to you, now. Oh—one other thing."

"Yeah?"

"I need the key to your cabin."

FOURTEEN

By the time I got to the gravel lane leading to the cabin, dusk had almost given in to night. The drive here had required more than my memory and, ironically, leaned on me glancing now and then at the original typed directions that Vernon Climer had provided me several days ago.

I had expected to encounter the blazing if friendly forest fire of color reminiscent of what I'd left back in Wisconsin. But traveling in twilight had muted those colors, and many of the trees were starting to show their skeletons through their gradually disappearing skins of red-orange-bronze-yellow-green, the occasional fat fir standing out in stark defiance.

I pulled the Mustang onto the apron of gravel where a Chrysler Cordoba, presumably Vernon's, was parked near the two-story cabin, whose downstairs windows glowed. I parked near the milk-chocolate vehicle with its dark-chocolate vinyl roof and Corinthian leather within, if Ricardo Montalban was to be believed. A luxury car to be sure, but a little smaller than many of its brothers, in response to the recent oil crisis and ongoing inflation.

Just the kind of car a businessman like Vernon Climer would select. No pink Cadillacs for him.

I headed casually to the porch, still in the black windbreaker and polo and jeans, but the .25 in my pocket had been replaced with my nine millimeter Browning. No noise-suppressor attached —no need out here in the boonies. Frogs were singing and insects talking, as they had when I'd been out for dinner with Corrie a hundred years ago, or was that yesterday?

Today, this evening, I was calling on her father.

I knocked. I heard but could not make out muffled talk behind that door—not right behind it, though—and, after I knocked again, footsteps approached and the door opened a crack or two. Vernon looked out tentatively, surprised that anyone might be calling on him—on them—out here.

He said nothing, just frowned at me uncomprehendingly. He was in a light blue shirt with darker blue stripes and a big white collar, unbuttoned and showing some chest hair and a gold chain, and if his white jeans had been any tighter, I could tell you whether he was circumcised or not. This was apparently Vernon Climer in casual mode.

"Sorry," I said. "Hate to interrupt your Sunday. But it's important. Talk to you for a few minutes?"

The narrow, sharp-cheekboned, sharp-chinned face considered me, sky-blue eyes slitting behind the oversize tortoiseshell glasses. His sandy hair didn't look so perfect now, mussed enough to reveal itself as more obviously thinning, the mustache darker and more Fu Manchu than porn star at the moment, tugged down by a frown.

My unenthusiastic host spoke softly, as if keeping this just between us. "How did you know you could find me here?"

"Leon told me."

It kind of sounded like, *Joe sent me.*

His eyes unslitted. "Leon has a big mouth."

"No, I'm just a charmer. If you're worried I might tell Max about this, don't be. This is going to be just between us."

"What is?"

"Our conversation. Should I come in, or would you like to join me out here? Kind of pleasant out on the porch. Cool. Nice nature sounds, if you don't mind the frogs croaking."

The door still remained barely open, but enough so that I

could see Dorrie Climer approach behind him. She was in a yellow-and-white halter top that her full breasts were too much for and tan hip-hugger bells that bulged a little over where the cloth cut her, but not in an unappealing way. Also no shoes, red toenails showing to match her fingernails and candy-apple red lip gloss. The hair that was neither quite brunette nor blonde was up in a beehive, held in place by a bright yellow scarf.

She was a good-looking woman. Or, as most men would admit to each other out of female earshot, one great-looking piece of ass.

The kind you might kill over.

She was looking at me suspiciously, then—as if going through the mental file cards and realizing she'd fucked me once upon a time—put on a bright red smile and said, "Well, hello, Jack. You want to come in for a drink or something?"

Her eyes flickered with friend-or-foe categorization, and hadn't made a decision yet when Vernon said to her over his shoulder, "Mr. Quarry and I need to speak in private for a moment, dear. Perhaps later."

Him calling her "dear" in front of me was a good start.

Then the door opened enough to let him come out and for her to be framed there in confusion, revealing some of the lines in her not-really-young-anymore face.

He shut it.

"Shall we walk?" he asked, nodding around. "Lovely view this time of night."

"Sure," I said.

We strolled to the edge of the property where brush and smaller trees fell to the shore of the Mississippi as if working to keep their balance. This time of day, or almost night, turned the river gun-metal gray; it had a nice shimmer, while—over the trees that crowded the opposite shore—sundown was burning like a distant conflagration.

"Why are you here, Mr. Quarry?" He was looking out at the river and the dying sun, not at me.

"Kind of a delicate matter," I admitted. "I have to ask your patience."

The face dominated by the big glasses swung toward me sharply. "If this is *blackmail*—"

I raised a single palm of surrender. "No, sir, it is not."

"Well, you clearly know about Dorrie and myself."

"I do."

"How did you come by that…knowledge? To that conclusion?"

Shrugging, I said, "I pretty much knew it that first day, when we spoke in your office, and Dorrie came bounding in without knocking. Supposedly looking for a check that she didn't really need to come calling for, since the post office has been managing that kind of thing just fine ever since Benjamin Franklin started it."

He returned his gaze to the river view. "Why not assume my cousin and I were putting her to the trouble just to be, well, assholes about it?"

"Two reasons. First, I saw no sign in your cousin Max's attitude, or his demeanor either, that indicated he had any real animosity toward his ex-wife-to-be. Second, you're too professional a businessman to be part of such nonsense."

Thin lips made a thin smile. "I suppose I should feel complimented."

"Maybe not. Another factor was that couch in your office."

"My couch? What the hell did you gather from my *couch*?"

"It was the only piece in that expensively appointed space that didn't match. It was oversize and looked very comfy, and obviously had a few miles on it. Perfect for banging a lush piece of ass like Dorrie on."

He took no, or at least little, offense at that crude characterization. Like I said, such things between men are tolerated and even expected. And anyway he was probably a little complimented by that, too.

I went on: "Then I noticed that you were having long conferences with somebody in your office. The Climax Club doesn't seem like the kind of place where you'd invite too many business associates in for a conference."

"And this was enough for you to somehow get Leon to talk."

"Yeah, it was. He was nervous because I figured out you were paying him to provide Mavis with smack, to keep her generally sedated."

He lifted the sharp chin, but neither confirmed nor denied my assertion.

I said, "But when Dorrie herself invited me to the Holiday Inn, to see where that great motel chain started… and also to fuck me silly…that got me to thinking. Why would she be so interested in me? I've been known to find a willing female now and then to fulfill my desires…but the nude model who was Mrs. Max Climer? Really? Maybe it had something to do with me being introduced as a security consultant. Maybe she wondered if I was here to investigate her. And you."

He had only barely flinched when I mentioned banging his honeybunch. But his eyes traveled back to me when I raised the issue of my presence in *Climax* world as a security consultant.

He asked, "Are you here to do that, Mr. Quarry? To investigate Dorrie and myself?"

"If I were, I'm not sure I'd have enough to cause you any trouble. Would Max be annoyed or otherwise freaked by the notion of the wife he was about to abandon climbing in the sack with his trusted cuz? Maybe. But more likely he'd just shrug. Maybe he'd even *like* the idea."

"That does sound like Max."

"But you're his business partner, the guy with a head for a different kind of figures than the editor of *Climax*. My guess is that you have systematically looted your cousin's company and plowed that dough somewhere safe, overseas maybe. This probably started when Mavis started sticking her nose in, and when Max started talking about expansion that was coming too early, adding new non-porn magazine titles and talking movie studio, and buying that Germantown mansion, wow—*that* must have been a bite."

"You can prove this?"

"Hell no! What do you think a security consultant *does*, anyway? Yale locks and security systems is about it. Of course, I'm not really a security consultant."

He was studying me now. "What *are* you, Mr. Quarry?"

And now I had to take a chance.

As long as I had that nine millimeter in my pocket, it was a chance I could risk taking. But if Vernon had received a phone call today from the Broker-like middleman he'd been dealing with, he might know about the two gay killers who died across from George's Truck Stop and Drag Bar last night.

Which would make the play I was about to make a very dangerous one.

Even fatal.

"I am going to assume," I said, "that Max told you about the kidnap attempt here at this cabin the night before last."

Vernon nodded somberly. "He did. But no details. He said only that you had handled things, and well. I had the impression that it was better for me not to know."

Just what I wanted to hear.

"That's probably so," I admitted. "But I need to fill in some details for you. You see, I am one of a team of three who were hired to *remove* Max Climer."

The chin lifted again. "By 'remove' you mean…?"

"Kill him, yes. My job was to infiltrate his business and offer myself in the security consultant role that you're familiar with. It's a kind of up-close-and-personal surveillance. I determined that staging a kidnapping would be an effective way to remove Max Climer—that it would be child's play to make it appear Max had been killed either because the kidnapping had gone wrong, or simply because the abductors had gotten their money and decided to kill their main witness."

He was just taking it in, eyes wide behind the tortoiseshell glasses.

I pressed on: "It was a botch. My associates staged the kidnapping, but in the process, Max's chauffeur killed them both, dying in the process himself. That left me to clean up afterward, dumping their van with their bodies in it on a backroad."

"Jesus," he said.

Did I have him? Was he buying it?

"What I have figured out," I said, "is that you and Mrs. Max Climer are the ones who hired this done."

His eyes flashed but he said nothing.

"Have you heard from our middleman about this?" I pressed. "Has he advised you of a Plan B?"

"No. No!"

I had him.

I finished the ploy.

"Then I have a proposition for you," I said. "Tomorrow, call your contact and say the contract is off."

"*Off?* Why…?"

"You don't need to do business now with anybody but me.

Your cousin trusts and accepts me. I have full access, and can bypass all of the new security measures, since I'm the one who had them installed. In addition, I will make it look like an accident, which will prevent this from ever coming back on you."

His eyes tensed. "You can do that?"

"I can and I will. That is…for twenty-five thousand dollars."

"But I *already*…"

"No worries on that score. With my late associates botching the kidnap scheme, you'll be able to cancel the contract and get a full refund. And I'm guessing twenty-five is less than you agreed to pay. That's probably what you put down."

"It…it is."

I nodded. "Let's walk back."

We did.

I sat in a rocking chair on the porch, and he sat in one next to me.

Gently rocking, I said, "I'm not asking for an answer right now. I'm aware I'm giving you a lot to think about. So sleep on it. Maybe talk about it with your little friend inside…"

He didn't react to that one way or the other.

"…and we'll talk tomorrow. And if we're in agreement, the Max Climer problem will be solved by the middle of the coming week."

He was rocking, too, not so gently. "I have to think about it. I have to think about it."

"I want you to. You mind if I ask you something?"

Hie eyebrows climbed over the big frames. "What is there left to ask?"

"Aren't you killing the golden goose? Isn't Max to *Climax* what Hefner is to *Playboy*, or Guccione to *Penthouse*?"

The rocking slowed and Vernon said, "He still *would* be. He'll become a tragic, mythic figure—who died for all our sins. But with him would also die his excesses and his bad judgment, and Climax Enterprises would be run as a *real* business…a business that can become an empire."

"You'd be the new face of *Climax*?"

He shook his head fairly vigorously. "No. Not me. Dorrie. A beautiful woman. The beautiful woman who was at Max Climer's side when it all began. Imagine it, Mr. Quarry—a men's magazine built on sex…let's face it, based on pussy…but with a woman ostensibly running it? A man, myself, of course, would *really* be behind the curtain…but think of the publicity, and the *cover* that we'd have any time the feminists come at us with pitchforks and torches!"

He'd almost answered my remaining question.

Almost.

I stopped rocking and stood. He did the same. I extended my hand.

"We'll call it a tentative deal," I said, as we shook hands. "And I'll wait for your confirmation tomorrow. Say, at the club right after opening?"

"At the club," he repeated, the thin lips smiling, "right after opening."

I went to the Mustang and glanced back, saying, "My apologies to your lovely friend. Tell her I'll take a rain check on that drink."

He lifted a hand in half wave, half benediction. "I'll let her know. We'll all look forward to a victory drink soon."

I got in, started it up, backed off, and pulled around to head back down the lane, watching in my rearview mirror as he stepped back inside.

Halfway down, I pulled over and got out, and headed back through the trees, not worrying about my feet crunching leaves. I made my way past the gas tank to peer into the kitchen window. Because there was one more thing I had to know.

They weren't at the kitchen table. But I could see that they were in the living room area, standing in front of the couches that surrounded the fireplace. She was listening intently and he was talking mile-a-minute, gesturing.

Still not enough.

I went to the window onto the living room area, at an angle where I hoped my peeping wouldn't be perceived. His back was largely to me, and he was blocking her.

Damn! Get the fuck out of the way....

As if he'd heard me, he moved just enough that I could see the pretty, pretty hard face with the bright red mouth and the blue-eye-shadowed brown eyes. She was listening, face alive with attention and thought, but only listening.

Then her lips moved and I read them.

We can trust him, she said. *I can wrap that little prick around my finger. He'll do it, all right.*

Not quite enough.

He was in Vietnam, she said. *He'll kill that son of a bitch and we'll finally be free. And all of it, all of it, will be ours.*

That was enough.

Then she embraced him and they started to kiss. He pulled her halter-top down, much as I had Corrie's tube top earlier today, and he buried his face between her breasts. Her head went back, liking it. This was a side angle now, and I had a fine window-peeker's view of them, not that I wanted one.

Jesus Christ, sex again.

She took him by the hand, her titties hanging out, and led him up those open stairs.

Maybe a minute later, I let myself in with the key that Max Climer provided, and the sound of them fucking, really going at it, came down the stairs. That must have been a loft of sorts up there, with the bedroom not closed off by a door. Because I could hear every moan and cry and whimper and grunt and even the sound of bedsprings. He was a lucky bastard. She was great in bed, as well I knew.

I just didn't have the heart to spoil it.

So I went over and sat on the couch with the nine millimeter in my hand, draped across my lap, and waited for them to finish. Maybe they'd come down and I could just take them out quickly, before they knew what hit them.

I had misgivings. I'm human. I'd made love to that woman, or anyway had sex with her, and the little time I'd spent with her had been pleasant, even out of bed. Vernon Climer seemed like a greedy, grasping louse, but he was also Corrie's father. And I liked Corrie—she was the kind of girl I could have been serious about in another life, and I hated putting her through anything shitty, even if she didn't like her old man much.

So I was just sitting there waiting for them to come down when I heard them talking, quietly, just some post-coital conversation. What the hell—I gave them a little time together. Then down those open stairs came not the two of them, but the snoring of both. It was almost comical, like the Three Stooges, but minus Larry.

You remember Larry—he died two nights ago on a lonely country road?

Anyway, I trudged upstairs, like a postman who knew he was delivering bad news, and in the big open room, they were at the right, in a vast round bed with pink silk sheets—Max Climer's bed, technically—snoring on their bellies with Vernon's hand draped across her back and starting up the slope of her ass. Between them on the nightstand were two after-sex cigarettes still burning in what looked to be a Climax Club ashtray.

Now if it bothers you that I removed them from the planet, it's always possible I didn't. That someone innocently left the gas on in the fireplace, turned all the way up, and those two cigarettes mingling in the bedside ashtray caused the explosion and fire.

At any rate, a hell of a fireball went up, just as I was reaching the Mustang.

And it's a good thing some responsible citizen found a pay phone at a diner just off the highway and called it in. Imagine if all those beautiful trees had been lost.

Now that would have been a tragedy.

FIFTEEN

I used my security-consultant keys to go in through the club, where its chairs upended on tables greeted me to the accompaniment of the smell of disinfectant, tobacco smoke, stale beer and just a piquant hint of puke. The second floor found the magazine office inhabited only by cigarette ghosts, and when I came up into the kitchen of the penthouse, as before, I for the first time found it occupied.

Max Climer, in his black silk robe rather carelessly slung around him, was sitting at the round orange-topped kitchen table. His breakfast was a can of Bud and a cigarette, and his unblinking blue eyes were staring at nothing, his black Caesar curls tousled, his baby face bland as always but with something haunted about it.

I joined him. I used the bottom of my polo shirt to wipe the security keys clean of prints, then tossed them on the table with a clunk.

"I won't be needing those now," I said. "I'm on my way out of town."

Looking past me, he nodded in a barely perceptible fashion.

"I assume you've received a phone call," I said, "about the tragic event."

Another barely perceptible nod, no eye contact.

I asked, "Do you know if anyone is on the way to talk to you? Cops, I mean? Fire department?"

His negative head shake also hardly registered.

"Someone may come," I said, "so I can't stay. I hope your cabin was insured."

He just stared past me.

"They wouldn't have suffered, if that helps. They didn't die screaming while they burned or anything. It was a big boom and over."

He swallowed.

"Anybody asks about me, my role as a security consultant ended Sunday. As we discussed, you don't know anything about me. You didn't ask for references and took me at face value, after interviewing me. Vietnam. Bronze Star. Give them all of that."

Another nod.

"Tell your niece that my job with you was finished and I got called to another one right away. That I heard about the tragedy and offer her my condolences, and she'll hear from me later."

Another nod.

I rose. "Is Mavis here? Sleeping in the other room?"

Nod. A drag on the cigarette. Some smoke exhaled.

"You need to accept that she's using. We're talking smack here, Max."

Now he looked at me. The eyes were red-rimmed, like Christopher Lee in a Dracula movie.

"You'll want to get her help," I said. "I cut off her supply, remember."

He swallowed and then finally spoke, nothing judgmental in the words or tone, merely curiosity, as he asked, "What kind of man are you, Quarry?"

I shrugged, smiled a little. "Just another loyal reader."

And then I got the hell out.

The Broker was pleased with the accidental nature of the passing of Max Climer's cousin, Vernon, and estranged wife, Dorrie.

"I appreciate you going to so much trouble," his voice said over the pay-phone receiver. I was back home in Wisconsin and calling in after the job, as was standard.

"I know," he continued, "that you make a point of not doing 'accidents,' that you are a more straightforward kind of craftsman. So I thank you. In this case, your discretion was well placed."

I didn't know how discreet it was, blowing up a cabin in the woods with a couple of people in it, but I said, "Thanks, Broker. But let's not make a habit out of these undercover jobs. I like a little distance between me and the guy I'm there to see."

That was euphemistic talk, something the Broker insisted on, even though his line was supposedly secure and I was in a booth using a pay phone.

"I understand your reticence, Quarry. But you are very good at getting close to people. Surprisingly so, since I sense you don't really like the human race very much."

"Yeah, well I'm stuck with it. We need to make arrangements for my payment."

"I'll send it to you Federal Express. That's a young Memphis company, ironically enough. You should consider investing. It's the next big thing."

I smirked. "Yeah, that and porno tapes."

Well, you can't always be right.

As for Max Climer, I never saw him again except on TV. Of course you already know the rest. How a disenfranchised member of Reverend Lesser Weaver's Evangelical Redeemer Church, reportedly unhappy at the phasing out of snake-handling and longing for more yaba-daba-doo holy babble, used a .38 Smith & Wesson Model 30 to blast three holes in Max Climer's belly.

Max had been standing outside a courthouse on the steps in Murfreesboro, having just won an obscenity case, and was boasting to the press about it, and telling how his empire was about to expand into more publishing and film production when Clovis Applewhite burst through with his .38 and his moral outrage. The assassin went down in a hail of ex-biker bodyguard bullets, but the editor and publisher of *Climax Magazine* took until early the next morning to die.

Like I said, gut shots kill so fucking slow.

Three months and a few days later, Mavis Crosby died of a heroin overdose in the alley behind a Florida club where she was dancing. The only national publication that noted her passing was *Climax Magazine*.

And not much at that.

In 1976, one of the last jobs I did for the Broker took me to the South again, and I broke a major personal rule, after the gig, making a side trip back to Memphis.

A new restaurant was going in under what had been Boyd's and my stakeout pad on the Highland Strip. And across the street, the Climax Club was no more. A fresh new brick facade had been put on, with only a few windows, and when I approached what had been the door to the club I saw written there in black-trimmed gold:

CLIMAX PUBLICATIONS
Deliveries in the Back

which seemed like the caption on a cartoon in the magazine.

I went in and found a businesslike brunette, attractive with dark-rim glasses and subdued make-up as well as a gray suit, seated at a yacht of a reception desk. It was difficult to make this space be part of what had been the Climax Club, but it was.

"Is Ms. Climer in?" I asked.

The receptionist looked at my casual attire, granted me a minuscule smile and said, "Do you have an appointment?"

"No, but I'm a personal acquaintance. She's in?"

"Yes, sir, but—"

"Tell her it's Jack Quarry."

I took a seat and, while the receptionist quietly passed my presence along, looked around. Wood paneling, black curtains—this *was* Climax Publications, wasn't it? Why weren't the curtains pink? And why were the magazines on the end tables *Time* and *Newsweek* and *Sports Illustrated*? Not a one carried split-beaver shots.

Very soon, Corrie strode out with a smile from a door behind and to one side of the reception desk. She was in a plaid sport-coat over a butter-yellow blouse with new denim flares and platforms; she was wearing glasses, big round lenses with barely visible frames. She offered a hand for me to shake, like I was an old business acquaintance. But I knew where that hand had been.

"So glad you dropped by," she said, the smile a little stiff and the words, too. "Let me show you around. Things have changed."

They had. A nest of cubicles where worker bees were typing took up both the audience area and the runway/stage space, though the bathrooms were still where they'd always been, as were the stairs to the second floor. She led me up and I enjoyed the view. That much of her hadn't changed.

The magazine floor was divided into offices with pebble-glassed doors, with an open area where artists worked on layouts and paste-up and such, the only thing vaguely like before. Corrie was about to show me into the office with CORDELIA CLIMER, PRESIDENT on it, when she changed her mind.

"Let's go upstairs," she said.

And soon, eerily, I was seated at that orange table again, this time with Corrie. She still had coffee left from breakfast and poured herself a cup. I settled for a caffeine-free Tab, which tasted just like Coke, if you poured it through a gym sock you found in a gutter.

I sipped the stuff as penance. "The glasses are new."

"Used to have contacts," she said, her smile a little embarrassed now. "These make for a better image, I guess."

"I, uh…apologize for dropping off the edge of the earth like that."

Her smile betrayed some of the hurt. Despite the businesswoman makeover, she still had the same pretty college-girl features, big brown eyes, button nose, pouty mouth; part of the current feminist schtick was no bra, so the perky boobs were reporting for duty, sir.

She said, "You really did just disappear. What was *that* about?"

I shrugged. "I don't know. Bad judgment. Immaturity. We were just getting to know each other and I didn't know how you'd take having a tragedy, like the loss of your father, you know, just…drop down in the middle of things. How that would play out. I guess I choked. And I really did have another job come in that I had to report to immediately."

She gave me a skeptical half-smile. "And in six months, you weren't anywhere around a phone?"

I lifted a shoulder and set it down. "I thought maybe an in-person visit would be better. Was I wrong?"

She shook her head. Her hair was blonder now, and that feathered Farrah Fawcett look had gotten to it. I didn't mind.

"It was a rough time," she admitted. "Someone as sensitive as you would have been nice to have around."

I managed not to do a Tab spit take. "You mean, Mr. Sensitivity who left you dangling? I am sorry. But you seem to be doing very well. Not to be crass about it…but it looks like you inherited everything."

She nodded, sipped her coffee. "From Daddy and from Uncle Max. I've made some changes."

"So I noticed."

She opened a hand. "Oh, there's still a Climax Club in town, and there will be half a dozen more around the country by the end of the year. But they'll be classy, lots of chrome and mirrors, first-rate food, pretty girls, no bottomless dancing, no—"

"Miner's hats?"

Her smile crinkled her chin. "No miner's hats. Do you still read the magazine? You claimed you did."

"Proud subscriber."

"Notice any difference?"

"Last few issues, the girls...that is, young women...are still quite naked, their thighs in no way glued together, but the photography is much better. Not so gynecological, but still outdoing *Playboy* and the rest of the competition. No Vaseline smeared on the lens, like *Penthouse*."

"And the politics?"

"A definite left-wing slant. Even a feminist one."

"Does that work for you, Jack?"

"Sure." Didn't exactly. To me they were trying to eat their pussy and have it, too.

She sat forward. "The political point of view is going to stay strong, Jack. And the sexual aspect will play up the equality of the sexes. More men in the photo shoots, erections and all."

I think she said "erections." With all this political talk, it could have been "elections."

"I'll give you a tour," she said. "Over half of our staff is female now. Our cartoon and photography editors are both women. The level of the writing, both in-house and from leading authors, is going to rival what Hefner produces, without losing our magazine's cheeky attitude."

Cheeky was right.

She folded her hands and leaned toward me with a pixieish smile. "So, Jack. As a reader...and an old friend...do you think my late uncle would approve of this new direction? He really was evolving politically, you know. And my father, I like to think, would applaud my professionalism. Do you agree?"

"I think so."

And I really did.

She reached across and touched my hand. "I *told* you I wasn't a prude."

She never had been, really. Corrie Colman—or that is, Corrie Climer—was a successful young woman, but in my memory, she would always be the girl who dry-humped me on her couch, like we were high schoolers under the bleachers; forever the sexy dirty little thing who thoughtfully picked up extra napkins so she could give me a hand job during *The Rocky Horror Picture Show*.

Of all the sex stuff I encountered in that depraved place known as Memphis, Tennessee, those innocent memories—innocent by way of comparison, anyway—would stay sharp while the debauchery I experienced and witnessed would blur into just so many more meaningless sexual encounters.

"*This* place hasn't changed much, anyway," I said, nodding to the kitchen around us. "Are you living here?"

"I am. Very convenient to our offices, at least till we expand in a few years. One of these days I'll remodel. Getting Climax Publications in order was the priority, and this is just a place to crash, admittedly a pretty decadent one. Maybe…maybe you'd like to stay over a few days."

"What did you do with the Clampetts' mansion?"

"It's on the market. Why, are you interested?"

That made us both laugh.

Then she got serious. "How would you like to do more than just hang out for a while?"

"Not sure I follow."

Her brown eyes were big and beautiful and as earnest as those of the nut who shot her uncle. "I could use a man, a smart man, who could stay on with me and build a new, responsible empire out of the old *Climax*. We could change the world, Jack, and get rich along the way."

I thanked her and said I'd think about it, but also that I couldn't stay.

"But, hey, I'll be back through this way again, before you know it," I lied.

Sure, it was a hell of an opportunity. A cushy life with a smart, beautiful woman. But I had a couple of sweet sexy memories with this girl that I didn't want to mess up. And like I said once, we all have our secrets, and one of mine was that I'd killed her father.

So, yeah—I suppose I've done some bad things in my life.

But I just can't see myself as a fucking pornographer.

AUTHOR'S NOTE

Despite its period setting, *Quarry's Climax* is not exactly an historical novel, and does not intend to suggest real people or events.

The Cinemax TV series, *Quarry*, imagined an expanded origin story for my character, including substituting for my Midwestern setting a backdrop of Memphis, Tennessee. By way of acknowledgment, and as a hat tip to writers Graham Gordy and Michael D. Fuller (who developed the show based upon my novels), I have taken Quarry to Memphis in these pages. While I spent a week in that city during the shooting of the series pilot, *Quarry's Climax* takes place in the Memphis of my imagination, the geography at times suggesting the real town and in other instances the needs of this narrative.

I'd like to acknowledge the following articles: "When It Was Hip to Be Square" by Michael Finger, *Memphis Magazine* (2001); "The History of George's Disco" by Vincent Astor, *Memphis Vive Magazine* (no date given); "The Night They Raided the Highland Strip" by David Dawson, *The Memphis Flyer* (2001); "Fear and Loathing on the Highland Strip" by Patrick Lantrip, *The Daily Helmsman* (2013); and the Historic-Memphis web site, as well as numerous other Internet sources dealing with Memphis and other topics.

My thanks to Graham and Michael, and to my wife and in-house editor Barb, as well as my agent, Dominick Abel, and Quarry's friend, editor and publisher, Charles Ardai, without whom the revival of interest in a character I created in 1971 is unlikely to have occurred.

WANT MORE QUARRY?

Try These Other Quarry Novels From
MAX ALLAN COLLINS and
HARD CASE CRIME...

The First Quarry

The ruthless hitman's first assignment: kill a philandering professor who has run afoul of some very dangerous men.

Quarry in the Middle

When two rival casino owners covet the same territory, guess who gets caught in the crossfire...

The Last Quarry

Retired killer Quarry gets talked into one last contract— but why would anyone want a beautiful librarian dead...?

Quarry's Ex

An easy job: protect the director of a low-budget movie. Until the director's wife turns out to be a woman out of Quarry's past.

The Wrong Quarry

Quarry zeroes in on the grieving family of a missing cheerleader. Does the hitman's hitman have the wrong quarry in his sights?

Or Read On for
Sample Chapters From
QUARRY'S CHOICE!

ONE

I had been killing people for money for over a year now, and it had been going fine. You have these occasional unexpected things crop up, but that's life.

Really, to be more exact about it, I'd been killing people for *good* money for over a year. Before that, in the Nam soup, I had been killing people for chump change, but then the Broker came along and showed me how to turn the skills Uncle Sugar had honed in me into a decent living.

I'll get to the Broker shortly, but you have to understand something: if you are a sick fuck who wants to read a book about some lunatic who gets off on murder, you are in the wrong place. I take no joy in killing. Pride, yes, but not to a degree that's obnoxious or anything.

As the Broker explained to me from right out of the gate, the people I'd be killing were essentially already dead: somebody had decided somebody else needed to die, and was going to have it done, which was where I came in. *After* the decision had been made. I'm not guilty of murder any more than my Browning nine millimeter is.

Guns don't kill people, some smart idiot said, *people kill people*—or in my case, people have some other person kill people.

There's a step here I've skipped and I better get to it. When I came home from overseas, I found my wife in bed with a guy. I didn't kill him, which I thought showed a certain restraint on my part, and when I went to talk to him about our "situation" the next day, I hadn't gone there to kill him, either. If I had, I'd have brought a fucking gun.

But he was working under this fancy little sports car, which like my wife had a body way too nice for this prick, and when he saw me, he looked up at me all sneery and said, "I got nothing to say to you, bunghole." And I took umbrage. Kicked the fucking jack out.

Ever hear the joke about the ice cream parlor? The cutie behind the counter asks, *"Crushed nuts, sir?"* *"No,"* the customer replies, *"rheumatism."* Well, in my wife's boyfriend's case it was crushed nuts.

They didn't prosecute me. They were going to at first, but then there was some support for me in the papers, and when the DA asked me if I might have *accidently* jostled the jack, I said, "Sure, why not?" I had enough medals to make it messy in an election year. So I walked.

This was on the west coast, but I came from the Midwest, where I was no longer welcome. My father's second wife did not want a murderer around—whether she was talking about the multiple yellow ones or the single-o white guy never came up. My father's first wife, my mother, had no opinion, being dead.

The Broker found me in a shit pad in L.A. on a rare bender—I'm not by nature a booze hound, nor a smoker, not even a damn coffee drinker—and recruited me. I would come to find out he recruited a lot of ex-military for his network of contract killers. Vietnam had left a lot of guys fucked-up and confused and full of rage, not necessarily in that order, and he could sort of…channel it.

The contracts came from what I guess you'd call underworld sources. Some kills were clearly mob-related; others were civilians who were probably dirty enough to make contacts with the kind of organized crime types who did business with the Broker —a referral kind of deal. Thing was, a guy like me never knew who had taken the contract. That was the reason for a Broker—he was our agent and the client's buffer.

Right now, maybe eighteen months since he'd tapped me on the shoulder, the Broker was sitting next to me in a red-button-tufted booth at the rear of an underpopulated restaurant and lounge on a Tuesday evening.

He was wearing that white hair a little longer now, sprayed in place, with some sideburns, and the mustache was plumper now, wider too, but nicely trimmed. I never knew where that deep tan came from—Florida vacations? A tanning salon? Surely not the very cold winter that Davenport, Iowa, had just gone through, and that's where we were—at the hotel the Broker owned a piece of, the Concort Inn near the government bridge over the Mississippi River, connecting Davenport and Rock Island, Illinois.

Specifically, we were in the Gay '90s Lounge, one of the better restaurants in the Iowa/Illinois Quad Cities, a study in San Francisco-whorehouse red and black. The place seemed to cater to two crowds—well-off diners in the restaurant area and a singles-scene "meat market" in the bar area. A small combo—piano, bass and guitar—was playing jazzy lounge music, very quietly. A couple couples were upright and groping on the postage-stamp dance floor, while maybe four tables were dining, money men with trophy wives. Or were those mistresses?

The Broker sat with his back to the wall and I was on the curve of the booth next to him. Not right next to him. We weren't cozy or anything. Often he had a bodyguard with him, another of his ex-military recruits—the Rock Island Arsenal was just across the government bridge and that may have been a source.

But tonight it was just the two of us, a real father-and-son duo. We'd both had the surf and turf (surf being shrimp, not lobster—my host didn't throw his dough around) and the Broker was sipping coffee. I had a Coke—actually, I was on my second. One of my few vices.

The Broker was in a double-knit navy two-button blazer with wide lapels, a wide light-blue tie and a very light-blue shirt, collars in. His trousers were canary yellow, but fortunately you couldn't see that with him sitting. A big man, six two with a slender but solid build, with the handsome features of a sophisticated guy in a high-end booze ad in *Playboy*. Eyes light gray. Face grooved for smile and frown lines but otherwise smooth. Mid-forties, though with the bearing of an even older man.

I was in a tan leisure suit with a light brown shirt. Five ten, one-hundred and sixty pounds, brown hair worn a little on the long side but not enough to get heckled by a truck driver. Sideburns but nothing radical. Just the guy sitting next to you on the bus or plane who you forgot about the instant you got where you were going. Average, but not so average that I couldn't get laid now and then.

"How do you like working with Boyd?" he asked. He had a mellow baritone and a liquid manner.

I had recently done a job with Boyd. Before that was a solo job and then five with a guy named Turner who I wound up bitching about to Broker.

Contracts were carried out by teams, in most cases, two-man ones—a passive and an active member. The passive guy went in ahead of time, sometimes as much as a month but at the very least two weeks, to get the pattern down, taking notes and running the whole surveillance gambit. The active guy came in a week or even less before the actual hit, utilizing the passive player's intel. Sometimes the passive half split town shortly after the active guy showed; sometimes the surveillance guy hung around if the getaway was tricky or backup might be needed.

"Well," I said, "you *do* know he's a fag."

The Broker's white eyebrows rose. It was like two caterpillars getting up on their hind legs. "No! Tough little fella like that? That hardly seems credible. Could you have misread the signs? You must be wrong, Quarry."

That wasn't my name. My name is none of your business. Quarry is the alias or code moniker that the Broker hung on me. All of us working for him on active/passive teams went by single names. Like Charo or Liberace.

"Look, Broker," I said, after a sip of Coke from a tall cocktail glass, "I don't give a shit."

"Pardon?"

"I said I don't care who Boyd fucks as long as he doesn't fuck up the job."

Surprise twinkled in the gray eyes and one corner of his mouth turned up slightly. "Well, that's a very broad-minded attitude, Quarry."

"A broad-minded attitude is exactly what Boyd doesn't have."

The Broker frowned at me. He had the sense of humor of a tuna. "If you wish, Quarry, I can team you with another of my boys—"

I stopped that with a raised hand. "I think Boyd is ideal for my purposes. He prefers passive and I prefer active. You're well aware that sitting stakeout bores the shit out of me, whereas Boyd has a streak of voyeur in him."

"Well, that's hardly enough to recommend him as your permanent partner."

"I'm not marrying him, Broker. Just working with him. And anyway, I like his style—he's a regular guy, a beer-drinking, ball-team-following Joe. Fits in, blends in, does not the fuck stand out."

Understand, Boyd was no queen—he was on the small side but sturdy, with a flat scarred face that had seen its share of brawls; his hair was curly and thick and brown, with bushy eyebrows and mustache, like so many were wearing. Also he had the kind of hard black eyes you see on a shark. Good eyes for this business.

With a what-the-hell wave, I said, "Let's go with Boyd."

Broker smiled, lifting his coffee cup. "Boyd it shall be."

You probably noticed that the Broker talked like a guy who'd read Shakespeare when to the rest of us English literature meant Ian Fleming.

"So," I said, "four jobs last year, and the one last month. That par for the course?"

He nodded. "Your advance should be paid in full by the end of this year. With that off the books, you'll have a very tidy income for a relative handful of jobs per annum."

"Jobs that carry with them a high degree of risk."

"Nothing in life is free, Quarry."

"Hey, I didn't just fall off a turnip truck."

A smile twitched below the mustache. "So, they have *turnip* trucks in Ohio, do they?"

"I wouldn't know. I've never been on a farm in my life. Strictly a townie." I leaned in. "Listen, Broker, I appreciate the free meal…keeping in mind nothing is free, like you said…but if you have no objection, I'm going to head home now."

He gestured like a *Price Is Right* model to a curtain opening onto a grand prize. "You're welcome to stay another night, my young friend. Several nights, if you like. You've earned a rest and a…bonus, perhaps? Possibly by way of a working girl? Something young and clean? Check out the redhead and the brunette, there at the end of the bar.…"

"No thanks, Broker." He seemed unusually generous tonight. "I just want to head back."

"But it's eight o'clock, and so many miles before you sleep."

I shrugged. "I like to drive at night. Why, is there something else you want to go over?"

It had felt throughout the meal that something more was hanging in the air than the question of Boyd as my official passive partner.

He lowered his head while raising his eyes to me. There was something careful, even cautious about it. Very quietly, though no one was seated anywhere near us, he asked, "How do you feel about a contract involving…a woman?"

With a shrug, I said, "I don't care who hires me. Hell, I don't even *know* who hires me, thanks to you."

"Not what I mean, Quarry."

I grinned at him. "Yeah, I knew that. Just rattling your chain, Broker."

He sighed, weight-of-the-world. "You know, I really should resent your insolence. Your impertinence. Your insubordination."

"Is that all? Can't you think of anything else that starts with an 'I'?"

That made him smile. Maybe a little sense of humor at that. "Such a rascal."

"Not to mention scamp."

Now he raised his head and lowered his eyes to me. Still very quiet, as if hunting wabbits. "I mean, if the…person you were dispatched to dislodge were of the female persuasion. Would that trouble you?"

That was arch even for the Broker.

I said, "I don't think it's possible to persuade anybody to be a female. Maybe you should check with Boyd on that one."

"Quarry…a straight answer please."

"You won't get one of those out of Boyd."

He frowned, very disapproving now.

I pawed the air. "Okay, okay. No clowning. No, I have no

problem with 'dislodging' the fairer sex. It's been my experience that women are human beings, and human beings are miserable creatures, so what the heck. Sure."

He nodded like a priest who'd just heard a confessor agree to a dozen Hail Marys. "Good to know. Good to know. Now, Quarry, there may be upon occasion jobs in the offing…so to speak…that might require a willingness to perform as you've indicated."

Jesus. I couldn't navigate that sentence with a fucking sextant. So I just nodded.

"May I say that I admire your technique. I don't wish to embarrass you, Quarry, but you have a certain almost surgical skill…"

That's what they said about Jack the Ripper.

"…minimizing discomfort for our…subjects."

"Stop," I said. "I'll blush."

He leaned back in the booth. "Not everyone came back from their terrible overseas ordeal as well-adjusted as you, Quarry. Some of my boys have real problems."

"Imagine that. I'd like some dessert, if that's okay."

I'd spotted a waiter with a dessert tray.

The Broker gave a little bow and did that Arab hand roll thing like he was approaching a pasha. Jesus, this guy. "It would be my pleasure, Quarry. There is a quite delicious little hot-fudge sundae we make here, with local ice cream. Courtesy of the Lagomarcino family."

"Didn't I do one of them in Chicago last September?"

"Uh, no. Different family. Similar name."

"Rose by any other."

Knowing I planned to book it after the meal, I had already stowed my little suitcase in the backseat of my Green Opel GT out in the parking lot.

So in fifteen minutes more or less, the Broker—after signing for the meal—walked me out into a cool spring night, the full moon casting a nice ivory glow on the nearby Mississippi, its surface of gentle ripples making the kind of interesting texture you find on an alligator.

The Concort Inn was a ten-story slab of glass and steel, angled to provide a better river view for the lucky guests on that side. The hotel resided on about half a city block's worth of cement, surrounded by parking. The lights of cars on the nearby government bridge, an ancient structure dating back to when nobody skimped on steel, were not enough to fend off the gloom of the nearby seedy warehouse area that made a less than scenic vista for the unlucky guests on the hotel's far side. The hotel's sign didn't do much to help matters, either, just a rooftop billboard with some under-lighting. Four lanes of traffic cutting under the bridge separated the parking lot from the riverfront, but on a Tuesday night at a quarter till nine, "traffic" was an overstatement.

We paused outside the double doors we'd just exited. No doorman was on duty. Which was to say, no doorman was ever on duty: this was Iowa. The Broker was lighting up a cheroot, and for the first time I realized what he most reminded me of: an old riverboat gambler. It took standing here on the Mississippi riverfront to finally get that across to me. All he needed one of those Rhett Butler hats and Bret Maverick string ties. And he should probably lose the yellow pants.

"Broker," I said, "you *knew* Boyd was gay."

"Did I?" He smiled a little, his eyebrows rising just a touch, his face turned a flickery orange by the kitchen match he was applying to the tip of the slender cigar.

"Of course you did," I said. "You research *all* of us down to how many fillings we have, what our fathers did for a living, and what church we stopped going to."

He waved the match out. "Why would I pretend not to have

known that Boyd is a practicing homosexual? Perhaps it's just something I missed."

"Christ, Broker, he lives in Albany with a hairdresser. And I doubt at this point he needs any practice."

He gave me a grandiloquent shrug. "Perhaps I thought you might have been offended had I mentioned the fact."

"I told you. He can sleep with sheep if he wants. Boy sheep, girl sheep, I don't give a fuck. But why hold that back?"

He let out some cheroot smoke. He seemed vaguely embarrassed. "One of my boys strongly objected to Boyd. But somehow my instincts told me that you would not. That you would be—"

"Broad-minded."

"I was going to say forward-thinking." He folded his arms and gave me a professorly look. "It's important we not be judgmental individuals, Quarry. That we be open-minded, unprejudiced, so that our professionalism will hold sway."

"Right the fuck on," I said.

He frowned at that, crudity never pleasing him, and the big two-tone green Fleetwood swung into the lot from the four-lane with the suddenness and speed of a boat that had gone terribly off course. The Caddy slowed as it cut across our path, the window on the rider's side down. The face looking out at us was almost demonic but that was because its Brillo-haired owner was grimacing as he leaned the big automatic against the rolled-down window and aimed it at us, like a turret gun on a ship's deck. A .45, I'd bet.

But I had taken the Broker down to the pavement, even before the thunder of it shook the night and my nine millimeter was out from under my left arm and I was shooting back at the bastard just as a second shot rocketed past me, eating some metal and glass, close enough for me to feel the wind of it but not touching me, and I put two holes in that grimace, both in the forehead, above either eye, and blood was welling down over his eyes like scarlet tears as the big vehicle tore out.

The last thing I saw was his expression, the expression of a screaming man, but he wasn't screaming, because he was dead. And dead men not only don't tell tales, they don't make *any* fucking sound, including screams.

I didn't chase them. Killing the shooter was enough. Maybe too much.

The Broker, looking alarmed, said something goddamned goofy to me, as I was hauling him up. "You wore a gun to *dinner* with me? Are you insane, man? This is neutral territory."

"Tell those assholes," I said, "and by the way—you're welcome."

He was unsteady on his feet.

The desk manager came rushing out and the Broker glanced back and shouted, "Nothing to see here! Children with cherry bombs. Franklin, keep everybody inside."

Franklin, an efficient little guy in a vest and bow tie (more riverboat shit), rounded up the curious, handing out drink chits.

There was a stone bench near the double doors and I sat Broker down on it and plopped beside him.

"You okay?" I asked.

He looked blister pale. "My dignity is bruised."

"Well, it doesn't show in those pants. I killed the shooter."

"Good. That should send a message."

"Yeah, but who to? And if you correct me with 'to whom,' I'll shoot you myself."

He frowned at me, more confusion than displeasure. "Did you get the license?"

"Not the number. Mississippi plates, though."

That seemed to pale him further. "Oh dear."

Oh dear, huh? Must be bad.

"Somebody may call the cops," I said. "Not everybody who

heard that, and maybe saw it, is in having free drinks right now."

He nodded. "You need to leave. Now."

"No argument." I had already put the gun away. They weren't coming back, not with a guy shot twice in the face they weren't. Anyway, by now "they" was one guy, driving a big buggy into a night that was just getting darker.

I patted him on the shoulder. That was about as friendly as we'd ever got. "Sure you're okay?"

"I'm fine. I'll handle this. Go."

I went, and the night I was driving into was getting darker, too. But I had the nine millimeter on the rider's seat to keep me company. That and my "Who's Next" eight-track.

TWO

Early spring in my neck of the woods is a pleasure. "My neck of the woods" isn't just a saying, it's literal: I owned an A-frame cottage on Paradise Lake, a shimmering blue jewel nestled in a luxuriantly green setting. In a few weeks, Spring Break would fuck that up, sending college students swarming into nearby Lake Geneva. It's a harbinger of summer to come, only with a nasty frantic edge that wouldn't kick in again till late August. Girls in their late teens and early twenties in bikinis are fine by me, but not when they smell of beer puke.

This is not to say that I wouldn't be taking advantage of the impending (how shall I delicately put it?) influx of sweet young pussy. I still looked like a college student myself, and had learned enough from books and TV to pass for one. So if I could connect with some cupcake looking to make a memory, why not help her out? Assuming, of course, I could manage that before she got shit-faced. Hey, I'm just that kind of guy.

But really the kind of guy I am is one who prefers hardly any people around. My circle of friends was limited to a few employees and regulars of Wilma's Welcome Inn, a cheerfully ramshackle lodge with a tavern and convenience store, within walking distance; a handful of Lake Geneva residents—businessmen in my monthly poker game; regulars at the health club I frequented; and assorted waitresses from the Playboy Club.

Mine was a monastic existence, really, except for the balling Bunnies and college girls part; mostly I lived a solitary life in my A-frame, sitting on the deck out back, watching the lovely rippling lake, where I swam when the weather warmed. I even had a little motorboat and sometimes fished. During the fall and winter, I curled up by the fire reading paperback westerns or watching television—I had splurged on a very tall antenna that could pull in the Chicago stations.

With the generous advance I'd received before starting contract work, I'd been able to outright buy the cottage and my Opel GT—my two extravagances. No mortgage. No car payment. Who had a better life than mine? Particularly in the spring, when ski season was over and summer was just a threat. Superman had his Fortress of Solitude, and I had my A-frame on Paradise Lake.

So when the Broker showed up on my doorstep, it seemed like a violation. Worlds colliding. I hadn't even known he knew where exactly I lived. The routine so far was that I called once a week from a pay phone for instructions, which were usually just "call back next week." Same Bat Time, same Bat Channel.

Only now, here he stood, tall and morose, in a peach-colored sport shirt, lighter peach slacks, white shoes…and no jacket! Imagine that. More casual than I'd ever seen him, but also rumpled, with sweat stains under his arms like a regular human. It was like he walked off the golf course in the middle of a round that was going for shit.

"Sorry to drop by unannounced like this," he said. Barely audible, his manner distracted.

I was in a t-shirt and cut-off jeans and probably looked like a beachcomber to him. I hadn't even carried a gun to the door with me. Never again.

A silver Lincoln with a vinyl top sat in my gravel drive behind my Opel GT, like an opulent tank about to fire away on the indigent. Behind the wheel of the Lincoln was a shrimpy guy named Roger who I'd met a couple of times. He was ex-military, too, but not one of the contract workers. More a bodyguard/valet.

The Broker saw me looking. "Roger will stay put, I assure you. I know you dislike him."

"I don't anything him. But you're right I don't want him in my house. Come in. Come in."

He stepped inside and I shut the door behind him. He just stood there, looking a little dazed. It had been just under a week since the parking-lot incident outside the Concort Inn. I had checked in once but got no answer. That happened sometimes, so I hadn't been overly concerned.

Still, the shooting had been hanging over things, a gray cloud threatening rain if not getting around to it.

Well, here was some rain. A whole Broker downpour. I stepped around him and curled a finger for him to follow and walked him down the hall past bedrooms and bathroom into the big open living room with its steel fireplace in the middle and kitchenette at left. The interior decoration was Early Dorm Room.

"Nice," he said, forcing a smile.

"It's nothing, but it's mine. Broker, what are you doing here?"

"…I need a word."

When did a conversation ever go well that started that way?

I gestured toward the fridge. "Can I get you a beer or a Coke or something?"

"Beer would be fine."

I pointed to the sliding glass doors onto the lake. "You go sit out on the deck. I'll join you in a minute."

"Fine. Uh, Quarry."

"Yeah?"

"Of course I know where you live. Why would you doubt that?"

Just like he'd known Boyd was gay.

"It's not that so much," I said. "It's just seeing you in…real life…that threw me."

He glanced around the space under the open-beamed A-ceiling. It was a landscape of throw pillows on the floor and one of the chairs was a bean bag. "Is that what this is? Real life?"

"Well, we don't generally socialize, you and me. Not on my turf. But I'll adjust." I gestured to the glass doors again. "Go on out. I'll get our drinks."

I got myself a Coke and a Coors for the Broker. He was sitting in one of the wooden deck chairs, looking out at the afternoon sun sparkling on the lake like a goddamn postcard.

"Really lovely," he said, as I settled in on a matching chair next to him. A little slatted wooden table between us took the drinks.

"I like it," I said with a shrug, slipping on sunglasses that had been on the table.

He turned the spooky gray eyes on me, enough glare off the pretty lake to make him squint at me like Clint Eastwood, if Clint Eastwood were much older. "We're not socializing, actually. Not that that would be unpleasant, but…this is business."

"Business like a contract."

His head angled to one side. "A contract, exactly. But not under the normal circumstances." He shook a professorly finger at me. "And I want it understood you have my blessing…or let's call it my 'okay'…to pass on this, this… opportunity."

"Opportunity, huh? How so?"

"It will pay fifty thousand dollars and all expenses."

That was an opportunity, all right.

I shrugged, as if unimpressed. "Well, you said it wasn't normal. So how else isn't it normal?"

An eyebrow raised. "You'll *know* who the client is."

That got a blink out of me. "We're breaking what-do-you-call-it, protocol, aren't we?"

"Indeed we are."

The Broker was one of the few people I ever knew who used that word in human speech. Not that there's any other kind.

I had a sip of Coke. "So who *is* this client?"

He looked out at the lake. "Who do you think I'm talking about, young man? Me."

That did make sense.

Somebody had tried to gun him down last week, and the Broker had been understandably shaken, and still was. I didn't know enough about the inter-workings of his business—hell, the workings period—to know whether being on the firing line himself was something that the Broker expected to occur, from time to time. As part of the price of doing business.

But I would have to say such an occurrence must have been rare, because six days later, the Broker appeared still to be reeling and, more than that, was right here smack in the middle of my world. The devil looking out at Paradise Lake.

"Obviously," I said, "this relates to last week's fun and games."

Slow single nod. "Obviously."

"And in the days since, you've determined who was behind that attempt."

Two nods, not so slow. "I have indeed. And I have your keen eyes to thank."

"Yeah?"

"That Mississippi license plate told the tale."

And then he told me one.

"For your own protection," he began, after two sips of Coors, "for the protection of all of those who work for me, I keep things on a need-to-know basis. Most of those we eliminate are from the world of business or perhaps politics, although never on a rarefied scale—we leave that to the CIA. Usually we remove fairly important people, because important people are involved in the kinds of affairs that can get a person removed."

"And not just business affairs," I said.

"No. Affairs of the heart, as well."

"Or the heart-on."

He didn't bother to wince at that, and simply went on: "You, *all* of you, are certainly aware that we do work for elements of organized crime—the so-called Mob. But your awareness is relatively vague. Again, you are provided intel on a need-to-know basis, while I protect you from interaction with those who have hired my...*our*...services."

"Okay," I said, trying not to sound impatient. I knew all this, but he was in a bad place, or anyway a strained one, and I wouldn't be needling him today. Much.

"One of the criminal organizations we do a fair share of work for is known as the Dixie Mafia." He looked from the lake to me. "Are you familiar with that term, Quarry?"

"No."

"It's not a phrase that indicates Italian or Sicilian ancestry. In fact, it's not a term that those involved in the group coined themselves—rather some newspaperman came up with it, to lend a little glamour to a rather slipshod enterprise, and this rabble embraced it. You will find in the so-called Dixie Mafia, for example, no 'don.' No 'boss of bosses.' Their roots are not Capone and Luciano, but Dillinger and Pretty Boy Floyd."

He explained that the Dixie Mafia comprised traveling criminals and roadhouse proprietors throughout the South—small-time thieves, bigger-time heist artists, car boosters, and con men; also, gambling- and whorehouse proprietors. Their only connection to the real Mafia was to pay a tax to the New Orleans mob, when on their turf.

"The Strip in Biloxi, Mississippi, has evolved into their base of operations," the Broker said. "It was a natural enough thing.

Just as the Dixie Mafia is a ragtag coterie of criminals, the Strip is a squalid patchwork of striptease clubs, shabby motels and sleazy bars. These provide the perfect surroundings for these migratory miscreants to meet, to plan their 'capers.' "

"If there's no 'don,' " I asked, "who do we do contract work for?"

He held his palms up. "Well, in recent years, one of the club owners has risen to power—initially as a fence and a message service, later hiding men on the run, laundering their cash, even investing in their enterprises…underwriting more ambitious heists."

"This is the man you've done business with."

He squinted again, gazing out at the blue lake, his hands tented. He selected his words. Then: "Yes and no. I've dealt directly with him on just two occasions."

His hands were clenched. Was that fear? Jesus, that was fear.

"Jack Killian," he said, talking to the lake. "From a surprisingly upper-class background. Chose the Air Force over college. Became a car thief who graduated to bank robbery. Once just another of those traveling criminals, if a notably sadistic one, now the owner of every fleshpot on the Biloxi Strip. He is not the don, not in the traditional Mafia sense. More like a feudal lord."

"But you don't deal with him."

He shook his head, paused for a sip of Coors. "Killian's partner, Woodrow Colton—Mr. Woody, he is called—is the Dixie Mafia's number two. The banker. The money launderer, the fixer, co-owner of Killian's clubs." He smiled, as if recalling a pleasant afternoon with a friend. "An amiable sort, Mr. Woody—who navigates through the political world of Biloxi, spreading joy. And cash. *He* has been my contact. And a pleasure with whom to do business."

I was hearing things I was not supposed to know. That none of us who worked for the Broker were supposed to know.

"And it is through Mr. Colton," the Broker went on, glancing at me with a faint smile flickering on the thin lips under the well-trimmed mustache, "that we have our avenue for…well, revenge is such an unpleasant word, and a concept for lessers. Let us call it retaliation. Let us call it self-protection."

"Let us call it," I said, "who do I kill?"

He resumed his contemplation of the lake. The sun had slipped behind some gently moving clouds that were making shadows in an afternoon suddenly turned a cool blue.

"Mr. Killian has ambitions," he said. "Perhaps he does in fact see himself as the 'don' of the Dixie Mafia. He has been buying up roadhouses in the south, in particular the rather notorious State-line Strip between Tennessee and Mississippi. And, as I say, he owns virtually every striptease joint, shack-up motel and sleazy bar on the Biloxi Strip."

"What does that have to do with the services we perform for him?"

The Broker was facing the lake but his eyes were closed now. "He has decided, Mr. Colton informs me, that he will henceforth handle all necessary liquidations 'within house.' That is certainly his privilege. I hold no long-term contracts with anyone."

It seemed to me that every contract we handled was as about long-term as it got, but I let it go. Honestly, though, "henceforth"?

"I am viewed," the Broker said, his eyes open now and on me, "as a loose end. The expression, however trite, remains apt: '*I know too much.*'"

And now so did I.

"So it's Killian, then," I said. "Point me."

He shook his head, frowning. "It's not that simple, nothing

so straightforward. There's a need for this to seem like something other than a simple hit."

"I don't do accidents."

"No, I know, that requires special training, and gifts that are not among yours." He had a healthy swig of beer. "No, I have something in mind for how this might be handled, but first it requires that you go…well, I suppose the term is 'undercover.' "

"Come again?"

There was a twinkle in the gray eyes as he replied—a fucking twinkle, I swear. "Mr. Colton has agreed to help us remove Mr. Killian."

"Could we skip the 'misters'? We are talking about killing this prick. And what makes you think you can trust Colton?"

He batted that away. "I don't think it's a matter of the second-in-command wishing to stage a coup—more that Mr. Killian and his roughneck ways…no matter how well he may dress, and I understand he is quite the clotheshorse…is making enemies in certain Biloxi circles of power. His behavior is so outrageous and so damned grasping that the politicians would very much like to see him retire. Or I should say, 'retired.'"

"A gold watch with a bullet through it."

"Metaphorically correct." He twisted toward me in the wooden chair and his hands were folded, resting against an arm of it. "There is an opening on Mr. Killian's staff of bodyguards that Mr. Colton is in a position to arrange for you to fill. That will put you very close to Mr. Killian. Close enough for you to gain his trust, or at least his laxity."

"Close enough to put out his lights."

Short, quick nods. "But he is extremely well-insulated, and this must be accomplished in a manner that won't embarrass or, worse, implicate Mr. Colton. Are you willing?"

"Like the Pope said on his death bed, why me?"

The Broker gestured in a slow-motion manner. "As it happens, you've never done a job in that colorful region. Never done a job emanating from that client. You are, after all, fairly new to the business."

"Yeah, you can't beat a fresh face. But what about the guys in the green Caddy the other night? You know, the one with the Mississippi plates?"

Both eyebrows went up, the white caterpillars on their hind legs again. "Well, one of them is quite dead, and the other was occupied, and probably got little more than a glimpse of you, if that, in that under-lit lot. Additionally, you were firing that weapon of yours, and I'm sure the orange flames it was spitting were a distraction."

"They usually are. I don't have to use a Southern accent or anything, do I?"

"No! You'll be a damn Yankee, but one recommended by the Number Two in the organization. You'll use 'Quarry,' and is 'John' all right for a first name?"

"Sure. Why not."

He damn near beamed. Staying in the wooden deck chair, sticking his legs straight out, he dug in a pants pocket and withdraw a fat letter-sized envelope, folded over. "Here's expense money, and a Michigan driver's license."

I took it. Two grand in hundreds, and a license with a picture of me—Broker had plenty of those from various states for this exact purpose.

But I frowned at him. "If you already had this ready, why ask if I was okay with 'John'?"

"Why," he asked, frowning back, "aren't you all right with it?"

"No, that's not the point. It's just…skip it."

My saying yes had brightened his mood considerably. "You'll need to buy some new clothes with some of that. As I said, Killian is a clotheshorse and he expects his people to dress professionally. That money should also be plenty to front a plane ticket. Fly into somewhere other than Biloxi, New Orleans perhaps, and rent a car. You can use any of your current identities for those operations."

There were many more details and we spoke into dusk. I invited him for a walleye dinner at Wilma's Welcome Inn, but he passed. He had a long drive home ahead of him.

We shook hands just outside my front door and he was smiling as he walked briskly to the Lincoln. Behind the wheel, Roger gave me a nod. I didn't return it.

I had a trip ahead of me, too.

I was fine with that—even if it was an unusual job that took me out of my element and meant I had to deal with people, which I didn't love. But fifty grand was fifty grand. So heading South was no big deal.

As long as the job didn't go south.